James Roberts Gilmore

A mountain-white heroine

James Roberts Gilmore

A mountain-white heroine

ISBN/EAN: 9783337184827

Printed in Europe, USA, Canada, Australia, Japan

Cover: Foto ©Andreas Hilbeck / pixelio.de

More available books at **www.hansebooks.com**

A

MOUNTAIN-WHITE HEROINE

BY

JAMES R. GILMORE

(EDMUND KIRKE)

AUTHOR OF "AMONG THE PINES" "THE LAST OF THE THORNDIKES"
"THE REAR-GUARD OF THE REVOLUTION" ETC.

———

NEW YORK AND CHICAGO
BELFORD, CLARKE AND COMPANY
1889

A MOUNTAIN-WHITE HEROINE.

INTRODUCTION.

OUR country offers hospitality to all civilized nations. It opens wide its doors to every man who desires civil and religious freedom, and is willing to assimilate with our people, and support our free institutions. It accords to him every right of property, and, after a brief proba- tion, the same voice in shaping our governmental policy that is enjoyed by our native-born population, whose fathers laid the foundations of our Republic, and who have themselves erected it into a great nation. But, like prudent householders, our native citizens do not give cordial welcome to the foreign beggar, burglar, incendiary, and cutthroat. And yet, recent investigations, conducted under the authority of Congress, disclose the fact that European governments are vomiting upon our shores their criminal and worthless characters in startling numbers. Their highways and by-ways are ransacked for paupers, and their jails and penitentiaries are emptied of dangerous vagabonds, to be thrust into our large cities in idle and lawless crowds, there to form an element that is a menace to the peace and security of any civilized community.

The presence of this element has already obliged every one of our larger municipalities to so augment its police force, as to greatly increase the tax-burden of its order-loving citizens.

This is an element sufficiently dangerous to cause alarm; but it is far less dangerous to us as an American people than those firebrands of Europe — the Anarchists and Socialists — whom foreign governments are scattering broadcast among us. The paupers and criminals threaten our security as individual citizens; the Anarchists and Socialists are a menace to the stability of our Government, and the integrity of our very civilization.

John Most, the high priest of American anarchy, in his recent examination before the Congressional Immigration Committee, expressed the opinion that there are fifty millions of Socialists in Europe, and he stated that two million Anarchists are already domiciled in the United States, and are being reinforced by every ship that arrives from the Continent. The number of Socialists already here he did not state; but they are undoubtedly more numerous than the Anarchists. When asked to define the difference between socialism and anarchism, Most replied that the Socialist seeks to change the whole system of society. He does not seek to abolish individual ownership, but — what is the same thing — he would have the earnings of property equally distributed among the people. Under this system he believes there would be no necessity for laws, nor any need of a government. Every man would become a law unto himself, and the State would soon go out of existence. The Anarchist, on the other hand, according to Most, believes in the equal distribution of all property, and the immediate and total abolition of all State government.

The mere statement of these doctrines is enough to show that these people are the natural enemies of our American civilization. They are simply destructives. License with them is liberty; and freedom the ability of the poor to pull down the rich, and to revel idly on the avails of other men's industry. Both Socialists and Anarchists are largely sceptics and atheists, and drawn, as they mainly are, from the most ignorant and degraded population of Europe, they are the ready instruments of designing demagogues who would build themselves up on the ruin of society. What enormities they would commit if once freed from restraint, may be seen in the recent developments in Chicago, and in the atrocities attending the great riots in Pittsburg and New York city.

But I conceive that the peril to which the country is exposed from this disorganizing element, lies not so much in its violent uprising, as in the peaceful spread of its opinions — the silent infusion of its poisonous virus into the veins of the great body of our working population, till they shall mistake French Communism, or German Socialism, or Russian Nihilism, for Anglo-Saxon freedom. The danger is that the country shall thus lose its national character, be un-Americanized, swung away from the traditions of our fathers, and from the English liberty, English law, and English religion, which have given us all our greatness as a nation.

This calamity may not be possible in our Eastern and Middle States, where the foreign element is a minority, and every school-boy knows that true freedom is liberty regulated by law, and its most characteristic trait a strict regard for the property and rights of other men. The natural field for these destructive theories is the West, where the foreign-born population is a much more potent element, and New England ideas have not so thoroughly leavened the community. In that section, which in the near future will hold the political power of the country, these atheistic and destructive principles are strongly aggressive, and gaining ground with astonishing rapidity. In Chicago alone there are now, according to Professor Samuel Ives Curtiss, forty thousand Anarchists, who openly counsel resistance to law, and support vile journals in which are reproduced the writings of Thomas Paine, the shallow utterances of Robert G. Ingersoll, and ribald parodies of all that is most sacred in human literature. These journals distinctly proclaim that property is theft, the future life a delusion, Christianity a fable, and God Himself merely a scarecrow, invented to keep the poor out of the rich man's cornfield.

All along the Great Lakes this fetid exhalation from the cesspools of Europe is spreading, and it threatens to soon taint the atmosphere of the entire West. And the misfortune is that the spread of the poison cannot be checked. No capitation tax will keep these men out of the country, and we cannot deny them a free expression of their opinions when they are in it. If we were to set zealously about the work we might convert a few of them to our political creed ; but the chances are that when we had made one proselyte two others would spring up in his place, armed at all points with false logic, and backed by the moral support of that European reserve of fifty millions.

But it is doubtful if any genuine Anarchist can be converted to our American idea of freedom. Hatred of the rich he has drunk in with his mother's milk, and the iron heel of the governing classes in his native country has so scarred his very soul, that he has come to regard all who are better-conditioned than himself as his natural enemies. He cannot be made to understand that there can be no tyranny where every man wears a crown, no actual inequality where all are equal before the law, no exclusive possession of riches where moderate intelligence, and persistent industry, will speedily bestow them upon the poorest and most illiterate. He is incapable of understanding this, and hence, is unable to appreciate either the rights or the duties of an American citizen. This being so, and these men increasing in number in a more rapid ratio than our native population, and every one of them having the ballot in his possession, how shall we during the coming years preserve our national character, and keep intact our American institutions ? The question is of vital moment to this nation, and it concerns not only every patriot, but every Christian who has at heart the upward progress of the human race, and would see his country achieve its high mission as the standard bearer of civil and religious freedom.

There can be but one answer to this question, and that is —*The safety of our American institutions depends*

*solely upon a more general education of our native-
born American population.* From our own people, who
have inherited our national traditions, and have our
Anglo-Saxon freedom in their very blood, must be formed
a body of intelligent, liberty-loving, God-fearing men,
whose ballots shall hold this destructive foreign element
in check, and thus preserve to us in their integrity our
national character, and our free institutions. Thus far
we have been safe in our numerical superiority; but with
this inflowing tide of socialism and anarchism over-
spreading all the West, the time has come when our
supremacy is endangered, and we need to be reinforced
by a body of voters who have the same ideals and aspira-
tions as ourselves. This reinforcement we must have, or
soon lose our character as an American people. This is
the emergency that is now upon the nation.

But where shall we look for an auxiliary native force
that will neutralize the baleful influence of this disorganizing foreign element? The Southern negro is the
born enemy of atheism and anarchism, and when his
rights as a freeman are more generally respected, and he
is better educated, and more fully acquainted with his
duties as an American citizen, he will be a valuable aid
in upholding our American institutions. But the negro
has not inherited our traditions, he has no ancestral mem-
ories connected with Bunker Hill, or King's Mountain,
nor does he belong to a race which through fifteen hundred years of blood and struggle has achieved enlightened
liberty and Christian civilization.

There is, however, among us a class of native-born

Americans, who, if educated, and socially and morally elevated, would I think give the country the added strength it needs to maintain intact its free institutions; and this class is the so-called " Mountain-White" population of the Southern Alleghanies. They occupy what is now the very heart of this country, and number about two millions, all of them native-born, with an inherited love of freedom, and the intense patriotism which is peculiar to our American character. Being either too poor, or too conscientious, to hold slaves, they were, more than a hundred years ago, forced back to the mountains by the slave-holding planters of the seaboard, and, insulated there, shut out from the world, and deprived of schools and churches, they have grown up in ignorance of their rights and duties as American citizens.

The present condition of these people is directly traceable to slavery; for in making the slave the planter's blacksmith, carpenter, wheelwright, and man of all work, slavery shut every avenue of honest employment against the working white man, and drove him to the mountains and the barren sand hills to starve and to die. And having there shut him out from the world, it legislated to keep him in ignorance, lest he should learn his rights and overthrow its power. Only a few years before the war I saw a planter of my acquaintance march twenty of these men up to the polls, and when they had voted at his bidding, he turned to me and said, " This is your boasted Democracy. These men govern this country: Jefferson gave them the right of suffrage, and they suppose they are voting for Jefferson now."

2

"But," I said to him, "why do you not teach them to think? Why not give them schools and churches?"

"Because, if we did, they might not vote for Jefferson."

This reply indicates the policy that was pursued toward these people, through long years, by the ruling element in the South. But ignorant as they generally are, there is not in the whole country a more honest, brave, and liberty-loving class of men than these "Mountain-Whites," and during our recent civil war they developed qualities that do honor to American manhood. Though citizens of seceded States, and hemmed in by secession armies, and a disloyal people, the majority of them stood firmly by the Union, enduring, for what they thought the right, such suffering as rarely falls to the lot of any people. Multitudes of them laid out in the woods, were hunted with blood-hounds, beaten with stripes, hung to trees, tossed on the points of bayonets, and buried while yet alive, rather than deny their country, or betray its friends. Grass-grown cross-roads, where rude guide posts point ways no traveler ever went; lonely mountain hamlets, unknown except to the census-taker and the tax-gatherer, where the spelling-book and the mail bag never were seen, produced a race of hereos whose deeds will vie with those of any of the most noted characters in our history.

Living as these people do, remote from traveled routes, they are seldom seen by travelers, and their exploits in the late war, performed as they were in small conflicts, and amid the seclusion of their remote mountains, have escaped the notice of the chroniclers of the great events that decided the fate of the nation. Nevertheless,

they are worthy of record at the present time, if for no
other reason than to show the character of a large native
element on which, when properly instructed, we may rely
to stem the tide of socialism and anarchy that is now
inundating the country. Therefore, it has been suggested
to me that I may do a public service by recounting some
of the war history of these people as it has been related to
me by veracious persons, and by drawing such a general picture of their way of life, and natural and social surround-
ings, as came under my personal observation during a
recent residence of some years in their near neighborhood.

The facts that I record were communicated to me by
some scores of individuals while I was traveling through
their country in pursuit of material for a series of histo-
ries of the early South-West, that I have recently written ;
and I had then no thought of ever giving them to the
public. I consequently took no further care at the time
to verify the various accounts I received than would be
natural to one who has more personal satisfaction in truth
than in fiction. But, since the idea of writing this
volume has been suggested to me, I have taken every
means of verifying its facts that are possible by a corre-
spondence with my original informants. The conclusion
I have arrived at is, that the main facts I relate are his-
torically true, and that, if some of the minor details
are not so, the fact does not detract from the truthful
character of my picture as a whole, nor render it a less
faithful representation of the rare heroism, and self-
devoted patriotism exhibited by these Mountain-Whites
during the recent war for the preservation of the Union.

CHAPTER I.

THE advent of a circus is a great event in the Southern Alleghanies. For weeks in advance of its coming, it is heralded by enormous placards posted at every country cross-road, and from far and near, for many miles around, the backwoods people gather to the exhibition. Often in some inconsiderable hamlet several thousands come together, and then, while whisky flows freely, ensue scenes of the wildest jollity, most uproarious noise, and reckless violence, from which a certain number of killed and wounded may be as accurately predicted as from the encounter of hostile forces in regular conflict. The secluded region among the mountains of Western North Carolina, which was the scene of the events I am about to relate, had never been afflicted with one of these equestrian visitations; but there came a day in the month of April, 1861, when the monster placard announced that the dancing dogs, the monkey that plays the tambourine, and the half-nude goddess who rides four steeds at once, bare-backed, and at full gallop, would soon be on exhibition in the widely-known village of Asheville.

The circus stole into town over night, and when the half-asleep dwellers in the place heard its measured tramp

on the highway, they knew that a long procession of
Mountain-Whites would follow in the morning. And it
did. One unbroken stream of both sexes, and all ages,
on foot, on horse-back, mule-back, and "critter back," and
in every kind of nondescript vehicle, poured into the
town, over all its principal thoroughfares, from early dawn
till high-noon; and I question if a like procession was
ever seen outside of the Southern Alleghanies.

With the first streak of day came an old negro, astride
of an antiquated ox, which was hitched to a two-wheeled
cart, laden with corn-fodder; and there soon followed
many a score of foot passengers. The men were in
slouched hats of all shapes and sizes, and the women in
the peculiar sun-bonnet of the region; or without any
other head gear than that which adorned our first mother.
The other garments of the women were merely a bright-
colored ribbon tied about the neck, and a gown of linsey,
or Dolly Varden chintz, such as formed the bed-curtains
of our great-grandmothers. The men wore the same
linsey, or homespun tow-cloth, and with both men and
women the garments, as a general thing, came only a
trifle below the knees, leaving exposed a bare ankle
of the precise color of the red clay that covered the
highway.

Following these pedestrians was another old negro,
mounted upon the forward end of a dilapidated wagon,
drawn by an ox and a mule, harnessed tandem, and urged
forward upon a slow walk by a long whip, which every
now and then, as the colored Jehu flourished it about his
head, became entangled in the necks of a bevy of moun-

tain beauties, who were seated in the bottom of the vehicle. Then came another platoon of " foot soldiery," and then two women riding abreast, one arrayed in bright colors, and seated upon a worn-out side saddle, strapped to the back of a two-year-old heifer, which she guided by a rope bridle, inserted in the mouth of the animal; the other, wearing a man's hat and boots, and astride of a mule, which she rode bare-backed, holding on one arm a basket of eggs, on the other, a young child, which was laughing and playing at hide-and-seek with a four-year-old boy, who was mounted behind the woman. Evidently, the eggs were to pay for the woman's admission to the show; the boy and the baby she probably expected to smuggle in gratis.

Then followed a troop of horsemen and horse-women, and in their rear, a large ox, bearing a young man and maiden, apparently in the first throes of courtship. He sat astride of the shoulders of the beast, his long legs nearly touching the ground; she behind him, in a more feminine attitude, her arm tightly clasped about his waist, and her finely-formed foot moving in regular cadence with the motion of the animal. Then appeared another woman in a man's hat and cavalry boots, riding sideways on a bag of corn; and beside her was a man with a head-gear adorned with a drooping feather, which had evidently been out in the rain till it had lost all its original erectility. They were followed by a clumsy farm wagon of the country, drawn by three pairs of gaudily-decorated mules, and containing at least a score of mountain roughs — great, bearded fellows, with enormous top-boots, which dangled from the ends and sides of the vehicle, with a Furioso air, which plainly said,

"Who doth these boots displace
Shall meet Bombastes face to face."

But I need not particularize further, where all was grotesque, and unlike any thing ordinarily seen in civilized communities.

The most of the people in this procession had dull, expressionless faces, and only a casual glance was needed to show that they were below the average of our rural population in civilization, and intelligence. A considerable portion had the appearance of well-to-do farmers, the remainder are known, far and wide, as "poor whites;" though they are not poor in the sense of being homeless, and destitute of the necessaries of life. However, their homes are often little better than hovels, and their food is usually a ration of salt pork, hominy, and "corn-dodger," which fails to develop in them a very high order of manhood. But the hovels are their own, and so are the small patches of cleared ground which they cultivate in the rudest and most primitive manner. Their "annual crops" are three or four swine, and a few bushels of corn and sweet potatoes. On this, and a scanty supply of game, they subsist — the potatoes, boiled and flavored with an iron pot; the corn, made into "hoe-cake," and baked in the ashes, or on the lid of a kettle fashioned for the purpose; and the swine salted, and smoked into bacon, and then fried till it has very much the same consistence as gutta-percha. This diet, no doubt, accounts for their generally sallow, cadaverous complexions, and for the prevailing absence of all spirit and energy for which they are distinguished.

This circus, with its "ground and lofty tumbling," was, to a majority of these mountaineers, the most interesting incident which had occurred in their lives; but it is referred to here merely because it brought to this secluded people their first intelligence of one of the most notable events in American history — the attack upon Fort Sumter, and the lowering of the flag of the Union before armed rebellion, in the harbor of Charleston. It is probable that not an individual in the assemblage had any adequate conception of the national bearing of the event, or of its vital relation to his own future; and yet, a feeling of dread and uncertainty, a vague sense of a grave crisis having come into their lives, pervaded the entire gathering, and sent each one back to his home pondering the tidings with more than his accustomed thoughtfulness.

By none was the political bearing of this event more fully appreciated than by three youths, aged respectively, fifteen, seventeen, and nineteen years, who occupied one of the upper seats of the immense tent at the beginning of the itinerant performance. They were of a better class than a larger portion of the motley audience. Their clothing was of homespun, like that of the others, but it was neat, cleanly, and well-fitting, and sat upon them with the easy grace which betokens good breeding. Their forms were erect, and their features clear-cut, and intelligent, with a frank, manly expression, and that look of unconscious dignity, which usually tells of an honorable lineage. And they *were* well-descended. An adverse

3

fate had condemned them to be born and reared in this backwoods region; but it had not deprived them of the qualities which come down in one's blood from a cultivated ancestry.

The circus exercises had begun at noon, and the young men had, for an hour or more, looked silently on at the performance — the gorgeous cavalcade, the bare-back race, the flying leaps, and the antics of the intelligent steed, which fires off pistols, dances a horn-pipe, and exhibits various other accomplishments that are supposed to be exclusively human — when the oldest of the three young men said to the others: "Boys, you don't seem to enjoy this thing any better than I do. Mother will want to hear this news — suppose we go home."

"I'm agreed," answered the youngest. "This affair isn't much; our pony can beat that trick-horse all to flinders."

"Then we had better start at once, for it won't do to cross the Ivy after sundown."

Dropping from the seats they occupied the young men then passed noiselessly along the rear of the benches, to avoid disturbing the audience; and, emerging from the tent, made their way to a clump of trees a short distance away, where, secured by his bridle to a swaying limb, the aforesaid pony was browsing.

As this pony performed an humble part in this history, he is entitled to a brief description. He belonged to a species that seems peculiar to this mountain region. Dun-brown in color, he had a coat well nigh as shaggy as a spaniel's. He was about fifteen hands high, with a head small, and shapely; limbs, clean and well formed, and haunches that were long and formed like those of a deer. He seemed too slender to possess much strength, but in his close-knit frame there was great endurance, and his eye — which was large and lustrous, but also gentle and coquettish as any woman's — told of unconquerable spirit, and an intelligence almost human. A rope bridle, a worn woolen blanket, strapped to his back, and a bag of corn, thrown loosely over his shoulders, comprised his accoutrements.

As the youngest of the youths — whom his brothers addressed as "Billy," or "Billy-Boy"— approached to untie the rope by which the pony was tethered, the animal raised his head, gave a low whinny, and then lifted his right fore-foot by way of salutation. The lad took the foot in his hand, shook it gently, and then saying, "give me a buss, Sam," bent forward toward the pony, when the latter instantly rubbed his nose against the boy's face in a most affectionate manner. These ceremonies over, Billy bounded upon the pony's back, and, turning to his elder brother, said, "Aleck, don't you think the bridge at Democrat will be fixed by the time we get thar?"

"No, I don't," answered the other. "The lazy loons won't have it done in a week. We must go back along the river."

"Then we had better be jogging, for by that route it's twenty miles to the Ivy." Saying this, the younger lad led the way up the road, followed by his brothers with the long, noiseless stride peculiar to the dwellers among these mountains.

They soon left the precincts of the town, and emerged upon a rolling country, dotted with woods and open fields, but well-nigh destitute of dwellings. Most of these cleared spaces were what are called "old fields"—land which perhaps a century ago had been planted in corn year after year, without any compost, till the soil became exhausted, and refused to yield any crop of more value than scrub-oaks, and a poor species of pine, scarcely fit for firewood. Through this abandoned district the young men trudged for half an hour before coming upon a single token of human occupation.

The first indication of civilization they encountered was a woman ploughing in a fenced-field adjoining the highway. Her head, arms, and feet were bare, and a soiled cotton gown appeared to be her only garment. She was leisurely stirring the weeds with a bull-tongue plough, drawn by a new-milch cow, while staggering along behind was her offspring, vainly trying to keep in the shallow furrow. As the young men came abreast of the woman, she turned her pinched face toward them, and, pausing a moment in her employment, dropped a courtesy, and saluted them with the universal "How-dy-e."

"Good morning," responded Billy, from the back of the pony, "Why don't your husband do that sort of work?"

"Oh, he's busy—got company—the barber's ter the house dressin' his har."

A few rods farther on they came to the "house," a one-story log shanty, about twelve feet square, with no visible opening except a door-way, and squatted in the midst of

a small clearing, which was littered over with chips, un-
cut wood, and all manner of rubbish. A little beyond
was the barber's shop — an edifice destitute alike of roof,
door, and windows. It was, in short, a hen-coop, set on
end, but still occupied by its natural tenant, and her brood
of chickens. Seated upon it was a ragged " native," the
very picture of forlornness; and kneeling on the ground
beside him, in his shirt-sleeves, was another "native" —
the artist in hair — who had trimmed the other's locks in
a horizontal "bang," and was in the act of combing them
straight down, in the latest mountain fashion.

"What is the price for trimming hair in this shop?"
asked the younger lad, as he rode by.

"A dime a cut," answered the artist, not looking up, or
altering his position, "An' we ax fools half-price. Will
you uns hev your'n done cut?"

The boy wisely refrained from replying, and going on
in silence the trio soon struck the road along the French
Broad river, and came in sight of the only dwelling of
any pretensions they had encountered since leaving the
outskirts of Asheville. Though living all their lives
within twenty-five miles of the town, only the eldest of
the three had ever visited it before, and he had gone to it
on that occasion by the direct road, that crosses the Ivy
by a bridge near the hamlet of Democrat, which now had
been recently broken down by a freshet. Every thing
was, therefore, new to all of them on the route they
were now pursuing. They had observed this house,
on their way up the river, and had wondered what
"lord of the manor" could have built so costly a

dwelling where his only neighbors were "mean trash"—apparently more deeply sunk in poverty and squalor than any in the neighborhood of their own home in the mountains.

The mansion stood on the lower ground bordering the river, and in general appearance was not unlike some of the better class of country houses of the last century, which may still be seen here and there throughout New England. A wide portico lay along its front, and its staring-white walls were ornamented with green blinds; but with these features, and its square, generous proportions, its resemblance to a Northern country residence terminated. Its other characteristics were entirely Southern, and of the era of slavery. These features were outside chimneys, going up at either end in pyramidal form; low log-cabins, surrounded with litter, and garrisoned by trouserless pickaninnies of every conceivable shade of darkness; a dingy barn, and a dilapidated rail-fence, that encircled the premises, and stretched back to broad meadows, and ploughed fields, which climbed to the very summit of a wood-crowned hill, far at the rear of the mansion. The highway was bordered by this fence, except on its lower side, where a dense group of alders and willows ran down to the river.

As the young men passed along the road in the shade of these trees, the elder brother said to the others, " I have found out who this mansion belongs to—Robert Vance. He was a poor boy like ourselves, but you see what he has come to—a wealthy man, and not much above thirty years old."

"He must have had rich friends to help him along," said the next younger brother.

"No, Benny, I reckon not," answered Aleck, "I saw the house his father used to live in when I was here a year ago. It's a few miles back of Asheville — a tumble-down log-cabin, no larger than ours, and the farm is not so good as our clearings; but his boys managed to get a fair education, with a year or two at the University. That, mother has not been able to give us, for she's had to struggle along alone, with no one to help her."

"A man can't do any thing without education," said Benjamin.

"There you are wrong, Ben," responded the younger lad. "Old Jackson couldn't even spell — so I've read in our history — and mother says father understood Greek and Latin, and was a graduate of the University, yet he died poorer than Parson Justin's mule."

"No matter what a man's education is," said the older brother, "he can't rise, or get rich in this country, without supporting slavery. Every one of our family who has risen to distinction has been a slave-holder; but father wouldn't hold slaves; and I think he was right. I'd rather be poor, and never heard of, than to live contrary to my conscience."

Nothing more was said that has any special bearing on this history, and it was not long before the young men arrived at Alexander's — a wayside hotel which, since the year 1826, has been a summer resort for dwellers on the sultry seaboard. Here they halted long enough to give the pony a bait from the bag of corn he carried on his back, and then they trudged on again.

For several miles the hills that bordered the river had been gradually swelling into mountains, and now the young men were in the midst of surprisingly grand and picturesque scenery. The narrow road — in many places blasted from the rocks along the water's edge — follows the windings of the river, which at this point makes a wide sweep, and opens suddenly upon a scene absolutely beyond description. A tall mountain springs, as it were, directly across the roadway, the broad river racing along at its base, its rapid current now foaming around huge boulders, now whirling in swift-boiling pools, now tumbling in white cascades over some sunken ledge, and then again, flowing on, wide, and deep, and placid, as if it had never known an angry mood in its whole career. And over all, are the high inclosing mountains, their wooded slopes, and bare sandstone cliffs, towering up a thousand feet and more, and often toppling over the very roadway, while every here and there a mountain torrent, fringed with pine, and rhododendron, dashes from its leafy covert, and falls broken into a spray of brilliants to the river below. For a distance of nearly thirty miles the French Broad has here ploughed a gigantic furrow in the crust of the earth, rending the rocks, and piling up the mountains in rugged precipices, and dizzy pine-clad slopes, of well-nigh unparalleled sublimity.

Along this gigantic causeway the young men journeyed, mile after mile, pausing often to take in the grandeur of the scene, till about an hour before sunset, when they

came to the Ivy, a mountain stream, now swollen greatly·
beyond its banks, and racing to the near-by French Broad,
like a maddened animal.   Two days before they had come
that way, and then had tethered the "dug out," by which
they had crossed the stream, to the limb of a tree.   It
was there still, but fifteen feet above its former position,
and entangled in the branches.   The stream was now
fully two hundred feet wide, and the current rushing on
at a speed that would have instantly swept the "dug
out" into the French Broad, and the most expert swim-
mer beyond the reach of human succor.   Crossing the
Ivy was therefore out of the question.

The boys were deliberating what to do in the emergency, when a couple of travelers appeared on the scene.
They were a man and a woman coming down the road.
He was tall and gaunt, and clad in seedy homespun, with
a half-filled meal-sack slung over one shoulder and a
short stick, supporting a bundle, over the other.   He
walked with a shuffling, faltering gait, as if fatigued with
a long journey, and unable to keep up with his more
energetic companion.   The woman was nearly as tall as
the man, and equally gaunt, but she came on with a firm,
quick stride, her limbs going at every step to the extreme
verge of a scanty cotton gown, that fell a little short of
her ankles.   This garment was of the precise color of the
road she was traveling, and of a piece with the limp sun-
bonnet upon her head._ Her feet were encased in a pair
of stout brogans, which, with her naked ankles, were so
thickly encrusted with mud that nothing short of a
modern deluge could restore them to their original con-

4

dition. Under her arm she carried a sack, from which protruded the handle of a frying-pan, while from a cord wound about her waist was suspended at her side, in the manner of a ladies' chatelaine, a battered coffee-pot. They were evidently on a journey—lodging in hay-ricks, or the open air, and with those rude utensils cooking their food by the wayside.

The woman walked a few paces in advance of the man, and as she came near, her thrown-back sun-bonnet disclosed well-formed features, a wealth of dark-brown hair, and eyes soft and kindly, but with a latent fire which showed she might explode on occasion. Still, about her mobile lips played a smile that betokened a genial nature, capable of enjoying a joke, or a hearty laugh, on any reasonable provocation. She was about thirty years of age, the man some six years older, and they were evidently married, or at least mated, after the fashion of their class in this mountain country.

The younger boy no sooner caught sight of the couple than he uttered a laugh, and said to his brothers: "It's Parson Justin and Sukey. Now, we shall have prayers and Old Hundred when we camp out to-night."

"Hush, Billy," said the elder youth, "don't make game of them." Then, as the travelers came nearer, he added, addressing the new comers, "Good evening, neighbors. You've been on a journey, I reckon."

"Yas," answered the woman, removing from her mouth the small stick in use among snuff-dippers, "been tu Rutherford to see my folks, an' we'se all tuckered out — footed hit thirty mile since mornin'."

"Thirty miles! then you must be tired," said Aleck.

"Tired hain't no name for hit," answered the woman, seating herself on a large stone by the road-side. "We'se dead beat, clean gin eout. If we uns was only ter home, the soft side of a plank wud bo as easy ter me as yer mother's best feather-bed." Saying this she resumed her snuff-stick.

"Well, Sukey," said the younger lad, "You can enjoy the soft side of the ground to-night. You can't get across the Ivy."

"We can't!" she exclaimed, "We shall. Hit's a long five mile, but we'll roost ter home to-night. Ye kin reckon on that."

"How will you?" asked the older youth, "the Ivy tearing as it is now?"

"Why, don't you know, Aleck? Thar's a crossin' a mile and more up the mounting — we come that way. A big poplar has fell slap over the run, an' ye kin cross on hit without the Parson sayin' prayers or axin' a blessin'."

"That is good news," said Aleck. "We had expected to camp out here till the Ivy had fallen."

"Waal I spect *ye'll* have ter, fur ye kant git that pony over. Nary four-futted critter bigger'n a bench-legged fyse (short-legged cur) kin walk that poplar."

"How large is the poplar?" asked the boy of fifteen.

"Hit mout be eight fut, hit mout be ten, an' some good Christian has hew'd off the top-side; but, my Billy-Boy, the gorge air a hundred feet down, an' no unreasonin' critter could keep hits head thar a minit."

"But, Sam is not an unreasonin' critter," responded

Billy, " he knows enough to run for Congress. He can keep his head where I can."

"He ar' a knowin' one; but try him on that track, Billy, an' ye'll be short a right decent pony. Ye'll land him in Kingdom-come, sartin."

" I'll risk him," said Billy. "What do you say, Aleck? Shall we try to cross up thar ? "

" We might look over the ground. Then if we can't get Sam across, I'll stay there with him over night, while you and Ben go on to mother. We'll let you lead the way, Sukey, when you're rested."

" I'se rested now," said the woman, springing lightly to her feet, and saying, " Come on," to the Parson, who all this while had sat as demure as a church mouse, and silent as a Quaker meeting. Without a word the reverend gentleman slowly rose, and with an unsteady step followed her, as, with a firm and manly stride, she led the way up the mountain.

The ravine through which the Ivy finds its way to the French Broad slopes on its southern side gradually up to the top of the elevated plateau which there borders the river, and the ascent at that point is not difficult. The path had been but little traveled, but a slight trail was distinctly visible in the coarse grass and undergrowth, and following this, the party were not long in arriving at the prostrate tulip, which in this section is called the poplar. It was a giant tree, fully ten feet in diameter at the butt, and, blown down by some recent hurricane, it had fallen directly across the stream, which here had forced its way through the solid rock, forming a channel about a hundred feet deep, broad at the bottom, but narrowing at the top of the ledge to a width of not more than twenty-five feet. A sudden depression in the ground afforded ready access to this natural bridge from its upper side, and the hewn surface of the tree would give a secure footing to man or woman; but could such an animal as a horse keep its head on the dizzy causeway ? and, if it could, how would it be got down from the trunk of the tree on the farther side, which there rested on a nearly level surface, and was all of ten feet from the ground ? These were the questions which the young men debated as they slowly followed the Parson and his wife across the bridge, and examined the ground on the opposite side of the Ivy.

"It can't be done, Billy," said his elder brother. "If you should get him across, the leap down would be sure to break his legs."

"But, I wouldn't let him down thar," answered Billy, "I'd walk him on to the first limb, whar it isn't more than five feet to the ground. Of course he can jump that far."

"What! take him fifty feet over that round trunk, soaked with the heavy rain of three days ago ?"

"I don't care if it *is* slippery," answered the boy, "Sam is well shod; and I tell you, he'll follow whar I lead. I could take him into the Parson's pulpit."

The woman and her husband had seated themselves on a near-by stump to await the result, and now she called out to the lad, "If ye try it, ye'll lose yer nag, my Billy-Boy. I'll bet ye a thousand dollars agin a hime book."

"You haven't a thousand dollars to lose," replied the
lad, "but if I don't get Sam across, I'll give you a hymn-
book — Rippon's, new about a hundred years ago."

Knowing the peculiar qualities of the animal the older
brothers now consented to the trial, enjoining upon
"Billy-Boy" great caution, and an immediate retreat in
case the pony should exhibit signs of fright or timidity.
Then the lad put his arm about the horse's neck, and
began to caress and address him very much as he might
have done a human being; the docile creature meanwhile
responding with every sign of intelligence and affection.
After he had thus established a sort of magnetic connection between himself and the animal, the boy took the
bridle in his hand, close at the bit, and breaking into an
evidently improvised song, led him on an easy, but steady,
walk upon the fallen poplar.

He had no difficulty in luring the pony upon the dizzy
bridge, nor a further distance of some twenty feet to
where the chasm began; but there the animal doubtless
caught sight of the deep gulf below, for a sudden tremor
passed over him, and he shrank back well-nigh to his
haunches.

"Back him off, Billy, back him off," shouted the older
boys. The younger lad gave them no heed, but, clutch-
ing the bridle more tightly, he lifted the horse's head
high in the air, and shouted, in a voice to make the woods
ring, the refrain of his song, "Over the river with
Sammy."

No longer able to see the gloomy deep below him, the
horse recovered himself instantly, and at a leisurely pace

now followed the boy across the ravine. At the opposite brink the lad ended his song, let down the pony's head, and with a steady stride led him along the unhewn portion of the poplar, which extended fully fifty feet to the first branch. Then he sprang to the ground, and, with a nimble leap, the pony followed. Once on the ground, the boy showered upon the pony the same caresses that had preceded the performance, the pony accepting them with all the delight a dog shows at the fondling of his master.

"I've lost the bet — yer the boy for me, Billy," cried the woman.

"It war amazin' well done," said the Parson, "Ye showed grit, narve, and ready wit, and hit's a drefful pity sech a boy shud be lost in these yere mountings."

"Thank you, Mr. Justin," said the lad; "but the credit belongs to Sam. I wouldn't have tried it with any other horse in Madison county."

Soon the party resumed their journey, and at the distance of half a mile struck the highway, following which for a couple of miles they came to a cross-road, where they separated, the preacher and his wife keeping on up the Ivy, the boys striking due north into the Walnut Mountains. In another hour the young men had received the glad welcome of their mother.

CHAPTER II.

PRECEDING EVENTS.

The father of the young men who have been introduced to the reader, was of highly honorable lineage. His family was of the old-time Virginia gentry, and for more than a century had held a prominent position in the political life of that State, and of the South generally. His grandfather had been an officer of the Revolution, and a personal friend of Washington; and like his other friends, Jefferson and Madison, he had been opposed to slavery, and in favor of its gradual extinction; and this sentiment had become traditional in the family, though all its members, who ever rose to any prominence, had been slaveholders. Being in Rome they adopted Roman customs, from, perhaps, motives of expediency, without questioning whether they were right or wrong.

But it was not so with Benjamin Hawkins. He was a man of strong moral convictions, and to him nothing was expedient that conflicted with his keen sense of absolute justice. He had no special love for the negro; but regarding him as a man, he thought him entitled to freedom. These sentiments he freely expressed, while yet a student at the University of Virginia, and, before he was graduated, he discovered that they had cost him the friendship of his own relatives, and of some of the most influential men in Virginia. He was known to possess talent, a ready eloquence, and great moral intrepidity, and — lighted candles are not safe things in a magazine of gunpowder. He had studied with a view to a profession; but he now saw that his opinions would bar his way, not merely to distinction, but to even a livelihood in any slave-holding community. And a livelihood he must have, not only for himself, but for a young woman who shared his sentiments, and had consented to share his fortunes. He might have thought of the North as the fit arena for one of his opinions; but his health was precarious, and he was told that a mild and genial climate was essential to his continued existence. Nowhere within the limits of the Union could such a climate be found, free from the contamination of slavery, except among the Southern Alleghanies.

That region he knew to be occupied by a rude and uncultivated people, who could afford only a meagre support to a member of any of the professions; but with his slender patrimony, he might there establish himself as an extensive planter, gain a livelihood from the soil, and at the same time, devote his rare abilities, and acquired knowledge, to the instruction and elevation of the ignorant and unlettered population by whom he would be surrounded. Thus, it will be seen, that not merely a desire for health and competence, but also philanthropic sentiment, led him to emigrate with his young wife to the mountains of North Carolina.

Buying there an extensive tract of fertile land, he built upon it a roomy log mansion, which he furnished with many of the appliances of an old civilization, including a

5

well-selected library to which he looked for companionship for himself and wife, in the dearth of social fellow-
ship that he anticipated in that isolated region. His house
he planted in a picturesque locality, on a gentle slope,
overlooking a wide extent of forest-clad country. Before
its door coursed a rocky streamlet, with the ceaseless song
it had sung since the dawn of time, and around it, " rock-
ribbed and ancient as the sun," rose the mountains, in
every variety of outline, and every hue of gray and blue,
in domes, and peaks, and pinnacles, piercing the clouds,
and soaring aloft till they seemed to touch the very stars
in the infinite blue above them.

When the scene was first looked upon by the young
wife, as the two sat together on the low verandah of their
dwelling, it seemed to her unapproachable in its sublime
beauty. The sun was just sinking behind the distant
peaks, gilding the clouds and mountains with burnished
gold; all the air was laden with the forest odors, and the
evening breeze came to their faces with an exhilarating
freshness, lapping their senses in a delicious dream, in
which they fancied that in a spot so silent, secluded, and
umbrageous, they might while away existence, forgetting
that weary heads and aching hearts are the heritage of all
the dwellers on this unrestful planet. But alas! the
morning brought them a rude awakening. The weary
heads and aching hearts were all about them, and vice,
and crime, and the lowest forms of animalism, held in
their slimy grip the larger part of that sylvan solitude.
In all that wide region there was not a single soul with
whom they could find congenial companionship.

They had looked for ignorance; but not an ignorance "deeper than ever plummet sounded;" they had expected to find its natural offspring, indolence and vice; but not indolence that was positive inertia, and vice unfit to be named, its fetid breath tainting all the atmosphere. Reared in a region where religion and morality, if not always observed, were by all uniformly respected, they had not conceived of a community in which they did not so much as exist — where grown-up men and women when spoken to of God, asked "Who is him?" where brothers intermarried with sisters, and husbands sold or bartered away their wives as they did their hounds, and women cast off their offspring almost as soon as they could run alone, and had no other feeling for them than that of the animals. To these lower deeps only a portion of the population had fallen; but the slime had so overspread the whole community that a near-by settlement had acquired the appropriate name of Sodom. They had happened upon, perhaps, the most degraded locality in all the Carolina mountains.

What struck the young couple with most astonishment was that these people, with scarcely any exception, were of the same blood as themselves — of English, Scotch-Irish, and Pennsylvania Dutch descent, which races have been the parent stock from which have sprung, not only the greatest men, but the most moral and intelligent communities, in our entire country. They knew that the first settlers of the region, as far back as 1750, were intelligent, God-fearing men, who, with dauntless courage, and determined will, had overcome the savages, and the

wilderness; and they soon discovered that many of these
degraded *proletaire*, bore the names, and were the direct
descendants of heroes who had fought under John Sevier at
King's Mountain, and smote with Jackson the veterans of
Wellington at New Orleans.   How then could the present
degradation of their descendants be accounted for? How,
except by their isolated situation, and their lack of civil
and religious instruction?   Shut out from the world, as
they had been for a hundred years, the Nineteenth Century had passed them by, leaving upon them not a trace
of its progress; and the slave-holding interest had legislated to keep them in ignorance — deprived them of
schools and churches — lest they should learn their rights,
and overthrow its power.

Shut out thus from the light, these people had abode.
in darkness, until at last they had lost both the will and
the power to lift themselves to a higher condition.   And,
as man never stands still — sinks downward if he does
not rise upward — so had they sunk deep and deeper into
a pool of slime until it had encrusted their entire natures.
But the living spark was still there.   Latent in them all
were the great qualities of their God-fearing ancestors.
It needed only the gentle voice of love, the Ithuriel touch
of knowledge, to lift them from out that slimy pool, and
to seat them clothed, and in their right mind, at the feet
of Jesus.

"What a glorious work it will be," they said one to the
other, "to acquaint these people with their rights and
privileges as free-born Americans; to give them a knowledge of God, and of their high heritage as His children,

His ministers, and co-workers through the infinite ages!"
How the heart of this frail woman, and this already death-
stricken man, leaped to the work as they looked abroad
upon fields laden heavy with unripened grain, and waiting only for the reapers to gather in the harvest! This
grain should not be suffered to wither and rot upon the
ground; it should be gathered into the garner of God,
and these two, lonely and feeble as they were, would be
the reapers.

So, this young man and woman went joyfully about the
task of educating and uplifting the poor people of their
neighborhood. She, delegating her household duties to .
an aged freedwoman who had come with her from Virginia, opened a school for their children in a wing which
was added to their log dwelling; and there she taught
them to read and write, and how to do well such household employments as would fall to their lot when they
became men and women: and he built a meeting-house
on a corner of his land, about a mile from his residence,
and there every Sunday, and often on week-day evenings,
gave to adults and children such simple instruction as
concerns every American citizen, and every immortal
being, adapting with great skill his teaching to their
capacities, and gradually luring them on to a higher
knowledge.

At first the novelty of the thing attracted the people
to the meetings, and they went away neither wiser nor
better for what they had heard; but interested by the
simple stories with which, after the manner of the Great
Master, the young man illustrated his teachings. These

stories they repeated to their neighbors, till the whole country within a radius of twenty miles had tidings of the new preacher, and such crowds gathered to hear him as overflowed the little building, and filled all the space around it to the utmost reach of his voice. Soon he saw the results of his teaching in children cleanly in person, and gentle in demeanor, and in men and women decently clad, eager to learn, and anxious to do their duties as fathers and mothers, and American citizens. In less than a twelve-month upwards of twenty couple, who had lived together unlawfully for years, were joined in legal wedlock, and this young man, without other ordination than that given by an earnest soul, and a peculiar fitness for the work he was doing, had organized a religious community of seventy members, and a Sabbath-school of still larger numbers. This he had done to hold these people to their good resolutions, to commit them openly to a better life, and thus to make of every one of them an instrument of good in his neighborhood.

Thus did this young man and woman labor, year after year, till a moral revolution was effected in the benighted community. And they had their reward, not only in men and women whom they saw "clothed, and in their right mind," but in the sincere affection and regard of all the country round.

But the zeal of the self-ordained clergyman overtasked his physical powers. The seeds of consumption were in his system when he left Virginia, and sensitive lungs are not strengthened by the extra effort of breathing the rare atmosphere of a region nearly three thousand feet above the sea. *So, at the end of six years, he laid down his work, and went to his reward, leaving his frail young wife to rear alone their three little boys, the youngest of whom was but an infant at her breast.

The young mother of three helpless children, who was thus, at the early age of twenty-four, cast upon her own resources, was no ordinary woman. In the summer of 1883 I met her several times at her home, and gathered from her the incidents I am relating; and, if I were to give, in the language that comes uppermost, the impression she then made upon me, I might be suspected of exaggeration. While relating some portions of her narrative she reminded me of the great actress, Rachel, as I saw her, on the eve of the *Coup d'etat* — when all Paris was hushed by the awful stillness that precedes the first throe of the earthquake — seize the tri-colored flag, and, waving it above her head, thrill and electrify three thousand Frenchmen with the wonderful Marseillaise. In form and feature Mrs. Hawkins was not unlike Rachel, only she was more queenly, more commanding. Art had not fashioned her, but nature, and nature when in the mood to produce a magnificent woman.

She was a remarkable person, and anywhere, in any sphere, would have exerted a deep and strong influence upon the community. When I knew her, sixty years had traced some deep lines about her mouth, and streaked with gray her once chestnut-brown hair, but there was still grace and vigor in her every movement, and a look in her clear, spiritual eyes, which told of a serene and lofty spirit, that might be bent, but could not be broken, by earthly calamity; for it was anchored "within the vail," where she lived, face to face with the Invisible. Those who knew her when she was young told me that she was then very beautiful, and I could easily believe it, for she was so yet, though her beauty was no longer of form or feature, but of the soul, which in repose looked through her eyes in a dreamy, faraway gaze, but when stirred by some thrilling recollection, would flash forth in a sort of heroic fire that blazed and scorched like the blast from a furnace. It struck me that a most intense, passionate nature had in her been trained, and elevated by Christian faith into an habitual serenity, which was never disturbed, except when some memory of the tragic past swept over her in a sudden tempest.

The calamity of her husband's death did not come upon Mrs. Hawkins singly. The aged servant, who had relieved her largely from household cares, also died at this period. Left thus absolutely alone to rear and provide for three little boys — the oldest scarcely five years of age, she was obliged to discontinue the school at her dwelling, and also all regular attendance upon the Sabbath-school, in the management of which she had been especially active. The services of the little church were, however, continued by the Parson Justin, who has been seen trudging along the French Broad road in the wake of his more energetic help-mate.

This man at the age of twenty-two, had been taught to read and write by Mrs. Hawkins, in her school for young children, and having a degree of ready wit, and a certain glibness of tongue, he had been found useful in

the conduct of the Sabbath-school. He was born, and
still lived, in a dilapidated log-house, about two miles
away, on one of the upper branches of the Ivy. The
building had been erected some fifty years before by his
grandfather, who, it was said, had fled to these mountains
to escape the penalty of some crime committed on the
seaboard. Here he remained undisturbed — perhaps because justice thought him not worth the following — and
here he bought a small patch of ground, built a roomy
log-dwelling, and went about raising small crops of corn
and sweet potatoes, swapping broken-down horses, and
over-reaching his more simple-minded neighbors.

In the course of nature he died, leaving his worldly
possessions to a son, who, even in this paradise of indolence, acquired the name of the " laziest man in Madison
county." He forced the Parson, when he was only a scrap
of a boy, to plant his corn and potatoes, and then leaving them to be strangled with weeds, this paragon of lazi-
ness would sit all day, pipe in mouth, in front of his door,
and hail every transient passer-by with an invitation to
join him in a smoke, with all the complacency of a great
landed proprietor. Magnificent timber stood in the forest not two hundred yards from his door-way, but when
his wife wanted fire-wood, he would tear a log from out
the front of his dwelling — for was not the edifice altogether too large, and this timber already seasoned? This
he did, log by log, and piece by piece, till the entire face
of the building had disappeared, walls, floors, doors, and
window-sash — all but the upper floor, and the two corner
posts that supported the roof; and those he might have

6

demolished had it not been too much of a task to climb
the ladder which led to the second story.

The result was that when he took his lazy way under
ground, and left his property to the Parson, the dwelling
presented a unique appearance, even for this region of
nondescript structures. Along the whole front was a
wide gap, without a window except in the upper story;
the huge outside chimney had half crumbled away, allow-
ing the smoke and flames to char and blacken the entire
end of the building; not a window was without a broken
pane, not a door hung upon its hinges, and the roof was
heaped high with heavy stones to keep down the puncheon
slabs which had been warped and twisted by the sun of
fifty summers. The grounds were in a like state of di-
lapidation — the barn an unroofed ruin, and the pig-sty
broken down, with the swine running freely about the
wretched patch of weedy corn, that grew at the rear of
the premises.

Into possession of this dilapidated inheritance, Parson
Justin came when he was twenty years of age, and he
had no sooner bestowed his father snugly under ground,
than, thinking "it is not good that man should be alone,"
he looked about him for a woman who should be ostensibly
his housekeeper, but in reality, his drudge and concubine.
Such an one he found in the energetic female who piloted
the Hawkins boys over the Ivy.

She was then a girl of only fourteen, but in stature already a woman. Somewhat sun-browned, she was still ex-
ceedingly beautiful, with a form fully developed, and ex-
quisitely moulded. She was as erect as a flag-staff, supple

as an eel, and graceful as a leopard, and she had withal an easy freedom of manner that rebelled at any control except that of her own wayward volitions. Her dark-brown hair was as glossy as silk; her eyes were blazing coals lit from some volcano within her. She was embodied restlessness, ever on the move, and taking no account of five-barred fences, or like impediments. Placing her hand upon the shoulder of a spirited sixteen-hand horse, she would vault upon his back, and race him about the country without saddle or bridle, giving no heed to stumps, or fallen trees, or mountain torrents. She was the very poetry of motion; but she slung things about in a very unpoetical fashion.

However, she had not been mistress of the place a month before she had reduced Justin to complete subjection, and the premises to a tolerable sort of order — the holes in the windows were closed with rags, the doors swung again easily upon their hinges, and the pigs were confined to their sty, and kept out of the corn-field. The interior of the house also took on a more orderly appearance, and yet, house-keeping was not Sukey's "gift." She preferred to roam the woods, rifle or shot-gun in hand, in pursuit of the deer or wild rabbit. With these she kept their larder well stocked, and sometimes she brought down game that would have been regarded as a trophy by a male sportsman — on two or three occasions, a bear, and once a panther, which had stretched itself along the limb of a tree, and was about to spring down upon her.

This couple had lived together about a year when the Hawkins family came into the neighborhood, and opened the school and meeting which has been referred to. With nothing else to do, Justin took it into his head to acquire the "rudiments of sound learning;" and having inherited the quick intelligence of his grandfather, it was not long before he had mastered the spelling-book, and got through the "National Reader." Then he exchanged Sukey's panther-skin with Mr. Hawkins for a Bible, and having floundered through a few of its pages, he regarded himself as a scholar.

Meanwhile, Mrs. Hawkins had become acquainted with Sukey, and she now urged upon her to follow the example of her husband — reading would be a solace to her in his absence, and enliven the time when they were together during the long winter evenings. One of Sukey's virtues was plain speaking, and she accordingly replied, "I doan't keer for solace, ma'am, I doan't use terbaccy that way. Bob does; I only dips. An' I doan't mind him bein' away — he hain't no company, the hounds is better; 'sides with such a lazy loon as him to find in vittles, I hain't no time ter read. Most every day, winter and summer, I has ter tramp it in the woods, an' when I gits home I'se too done gone tired ter holt my head up."

Not long after Mr. Hawkins began the Sunday meetings, Justin received "serious impressions?"— had some slight pains in the region of the stomach — and going home he said to Sukey, laying his hand on the spot, "I feels awful bad round yere, Sukey; that shows I'se gettin' religion."

"Wa'll," said Sukey, "I hopes hit will do yer good — suthink'll have ter, or ye'll never be a man."

After awhile Justin blossomed out a full-blown convert, and applied to Mr. Hawkins to be enrolled among the members of his community — church it could scarcely be called, for he taught no creed, and, not being ordained, practised no baptism. To this Mr. Hawkins objected so long as Justin lived in unholy relations with Sukey — the thing, he said, was in every way scandalous, and they ought to be married. Thereupon Justin proposed to Sukey to go with him to Marshall, and be spliced in civilized fashion. This the woman bluntly refused to do, insinuating pretty plainly that she was even then looking about for "another feller," and Justin would very soon have to kill his own venison. Really alarmed, he reported her refusal at once to Mr. Hawkins, expressing, however, concern for Sukey's soul, and not fear for the threatened shortage in his supply of daily provender.

The situation being made known to Mrs. Hawkins, she mounted her horse, and rode over to Justin's "plantation." The gentle woman, by her kindly ways, had already won the heart of the untamed daughter of the woods; this she knew, and consequently she felt sure of a friendly welcome. In this she was not disappointed. She had no sooner opened the door than Sukey's expressive features lighted up, and dropping the garment she was trying, for perhaps the fiftieth time, to patch, she grasped Mrs. Hawkins by the hand, and exclaimed, "I'se right glad ter see ye, ma'am; hit's good for sore eyes an' a sore heart — hit's loike a bit o' the sun shinin' down inter the deep ravine along the Ivy."

Mrs. Hawkins responded kindly to this greeting, and soon opened the subject she had come to talk about. It was wrong, she said, for Sukey and Justin to live together as they were living. Sukey should marry him to take away the disgrace from herself, and to strengthen the good resolutions he had formed to lead a better life,— which he could not do, if he continued to live in such a relation with her as was not sanctioned by either the law or the Christian religion..

Sukey heard her through without remark, and then answered, gravely, " I doan't set no valu' on his good resolutions, ma'am, an' ye moutn't if ye know'd him as I does. He's just loike what they say uv his farder and gran'ther — lazy as one, an' as big a thief as t'other. Why, he steals game thet I gits by all-day hunting; and swops hit off for bacon. He'd ruther pay twenty cents a pound for greasy swine-flesh, nor eat my best venison for nothin'. An' the swine ar' got inter his blood — made him just loike the porkers, an' thet's the trouble with all the folks round yere. They'se lived on swine so long that they'se got to be swine tharselves. But, ye say true, ma'am, hit's a disgrace for me to live with him as folks thinks I does live. I take shame to myself for ever doin' hit — not 'case the Parson, nor the Justice, never said a few words over us; but 'case I lowered myself ter live with such a man. No one ever told me afore that hit war wrong. All the folks round yere does the loikes. But, I doan't live so now. Soon as I found him out I said to him, 'Thet ar' yer side uv the house, an' this ar' is mine, an' hit won't be healthy for ye ter step over the

line atween us.' He hain't tried to, fur with all the rest,
he's a durn'd coward. Now, he's comin' this marryin'
dodge jest ter git me ter live with him agin; thet ar' the
meanin' o' the hull uv hit — Sunday meetin' an' all.
But hit won't work. The minit we was spliced I
couldn't holp myself. No, ma'am, I'd sooner be a slave-
nigger, nor be tied for life ter such a man."

Seeing that further argument would be of no avail, and
questioning much if the poor girl were not right in refusing to be the wife of Justin, Mrs. Hawkins said nothing
more, except to ask Sukey to come and visit her whenever
she had leisure to do so.

"Do ye mean thet, ma'am!" exclaimed the girl.
"Does yer know how much I want ter come ter ye! how
I never yere yer voice, or git one uv yer kind looks, but
hit stirs me all through and through, lifts me up loike,
an' makes me long ter be better. I'se a pore ignurant
girl, ma'am, as never had no bringin' up, but if I could
once in a while talk ter ye, I might larn suthin', I might
grow to be a good woman."

With a warm pressure of the hand, Mrs. Hawkins
answered, "Come to me often, Sukey; you can't come
too often, I shall always be glad to see you, and in every
way I will do all I can for you."

Soon after this Sukey joined the school, and then became a regular attendant upon the Sunday meetings, and
it was not many months before the patient love and
kindness of Mrs. Hawkins had made of this wild waif of
the forest a new creature. Of course, she did not all at
once lay aside her uncouth ways, and become a model of

propriety and refinement, for how could she cast off in a moment the habits of a life-time? But day by day she was seen to be more tidy in her apparel, more refined in her manners, more gentle in her deportment, and soon she came to a fixed resolve to lead a new life, and be a true woman.

Justin also gave evidence of real amendment. His treatment of Sukey became especially kind and considerate. He had never before thought of relieving her from any portion of the household drudgery, but now he rose betimes to build the fire, fetch the water, cut and carry in the wood, and he even swept the floors, made his own bed, and set to rights his own bedroom. After the manner of his lazy sire, he had been accustomed to pass much of his time sitting idly before the door-way, tainting the air with clouds of cheap tobacco; but now his pipe was reserved for rare occasions, and this wasted time was expended in repairing the fences, hoeing the corn, and putting a new roof upon the ancient barn, to render it a fit shelter for a neglected horse, which heretofore, winter and summer, had known no other lodging-place than the open air of the forest. This horse had till now been suffered, as had Sukey, to get its livelihood by its own industry; but now it was provided with fodder, and Justin even went so far as to rub it down with a wisp of straw — a curry-comb being a thing unknown in that particular locality. The result was, the creature got some flesh upon its ribs, some gloss upon its coat, and some spirit into its soul — that is, if it had a soul, and I suppose it had, if the term be restricted to so much of the thinking principle as cognizes, and takes thought of, the relations of sensible objects.

Soon, through all the country round, the moral revolution which had been wrought in this man was known, and remarked upon; and so, he became like a lantern in a dark night, like a bon-fire upon a mountain-top, and men said to one another, "If the Parson's talk kin fotch sich a change inter such a critter as Bob Justin, thar must be suthin' in them ar' meetin's."

All this may have indicated a positive and genuine reformation of character, or it may have resulted from the fact that in the Bible, which Justin had bought with the panther-robe stolen from Sukey, he had read the story of the patriarch Jacob — how he worked seven years for a wife, and then, getting cheated, worked another seven years for that same damsel, who by that time must have gotten pretty well along in life — older by half than Sukey — and, perhaps, not half so beautiful. Now, it must not be supposed that Justin had the most distant resemblance to Jacob. He had neither his shrewdness, his pastoral knowledge, nor yet, the patient persistence with which for fourteen years the old patriarch followed up a commendable purpose. But, where Jacob had worked years for Rachel, might not Justin work months for Sukey. She was certainly worth that amount of effort now that her face was washed, her hair combed, her attire made more becoming, and her wild nature tamed to absolute gentleness, by the loving influence of Mrs. Hawkins. I do not affirm that this was actually the case, I only know that before half of fourteen months had elapsed,

7

the poor unsophisticated girl said to that lady, "I can't love him, ma'am, I'se tried ter, but I can't. Perhaps I mout if he'd allers been as kind, and patient, an' gentle as he ar' now; but, whenever I tries ter feel right ter him, thar comes up ter me his old loungin' ways, his lazy keer for his own carcus, and his low down sperrit — mean enuff ter be cowed by a woman. Hit ar' sartin that he ar' another man, an' hit mout be, that I orter marry him to keep him so. Won't ye tole me what to do, ma'am?"

Mrs. Hawkins declined to advise Sukey in a matter of such vital moment to her whole future; but she said decidedly that she could not with propriety live any longer with Justin without becoming his wife — it might be right in itself, it might escape censure from that community, but it bore the appearance of evil, and that should be avoided by all who tried to lead a Christian life.

Thus it came about that Justin attained his object, and Sukey, having made one great mistake, made, in consequence of it, another and a greater. Deeply she regretted it; with bitter tears she sought some way to free herself from her thraldom, but she found none; and so, worn in body, and weary of soul, she carried that chain to the end of her days. Alas! she sadly learned that the entrance of evil is like the flowing in of waters — the sluice-gate once opened, the floods pour in, and the whole life is overwhelmed by the deluge.

But Sukey held her peace, disclosing her misery not even to Mrs. Hawkins; and thus it was that Justin, though he habitually snarled like a wolf, or growled like a bear, at home, could venture abroad undetected, while arrayed, as he always was, in a well-fitting suit of sheep's clothing. He even had the address to pass his counterfeit piety upon Mrs. Hawkins, and thereby to succeed her husband in his ministry at the little meeting-house. The pay was poor — a few bags of corn-meal, and a few bushels of sweet potatoes — but the preaching was not much better, and all the good there was in it, cost him no effort ; for it was derived from Mrs. Hawkins, who "coached" him regularly every Saturday. Thus with Sukey to make not less than three hunting excursions a week, he could let the weeds grow up in his garden, and go about his "parish" in indolent ease, a "shining light," a "moral miracle"—all which he was, and something more, as will appear farther on in this history.

The fifteen years that followed the death of her husband flowed on in the life of Mrs. Hawkins in a placid stream, without a ripple, or a single noteworthy obstruction. Her boys grew up all that she would have them — manly, pure-hearted, high-principled, and devotedly attached to her, and to one another ; and though she shrank from publicity, and never appeared even in the little meeting-house except as a listener, she continued to be a moral force which gave most of its real vitality to the whole of this mountain neighborhood. By all these people she was regarded with a respect that bordered upon veneration, and though she never obtruded upon them her opinions on public affairs, her counsel was sought, and her advice followed, in all matters of concern to the rustic community. Such was the condition of things when news arrived that war had broken out in Charleston Harbor, and this preliminary statement has seemed necessary to a clear understanding of the events that followed.

CHAPTER III.

THE CAPTURE OF ELLIS.

LIKE a fire through a prairie the news of the fall of Fort Sumter swept through all that mountain region, creating a general panic; but when the first alarm was over, the people of the district settled down into a quiet conviction that the conflagration would not reach their borders. Seven States had already seceded, but they deemed North Carolina fast anchored in the Union, and had no fear that she would slip her cable, and drift out into the tempest. But the State did secede, and tidings of the event reached Marshall, the county seat of Madison county, in the latter part of May, a little more than a month after the fall of Fort Sumter.

These tidings were heard by a tall man, mounted upon a large, raw-boned horse, who had just entered the town, and was about to alight at the Court-House, around which was gathered the numerous crowd that, in this region, always attends a session of the Court. This man listened attentively to the news, asked a few questions of the bystanders, and then turned his horse's head as if about to ride away. As he did so, some one near him asked, "G'wine ter leave, Reuben? Thor't ye hed a case 'fore the Court."

"Well, I have," he answered, "but it won't come on till this murder trial is over. I prefer being home to lounging 'round here."

Saying this he rode briskly down the river road, to where another road, branching from it on the right, leads to Warm Springs over the Walnut Mountains.   Here he halted at a blacksmith's shop, while the smith fastened the shoes of his horse, and then at a rapid pace, he rode up the steep and rugged highway that there climbs the mountain.

He seemed a man of about thirty years, and, though clad in homespun, was of striking appearance, and evidently of a higher intelligence than the motley crowd he had left at the Court-House.   He was of large stature, with a deep chest, broad shoulders, long and muscular arms, and a large head, covered by a slouched-hat from underneath which escaped a heavy mass of glossy black hair.   His beard, which had apparently never known a razor, covered the whole of his face except his high cheek-bones, a prominent nose, and eyes that were large, deeply black, and of a peculiar intensity.   He sat his horse with the ease peculiar to these mountain people, and his whole bearing indicated the conscious power that usually accompanies more than common mental or physical ability.

About three miles up the road he came to what is known as Walnut Creek, and there, turning sharply to the left, he rode rapidly on by a narrow lane to a log-house, at the brow of the mountain, overlooking the French Broad, and, by an air line, not more than a mile and a half distant from the Court-House whence he had started.   As his horse's feet sounded on the path leading to the house, a comely, tidily-dressed woman came to the door-way, and said to him, "What! ar ye back so soon, Reuben?"

"Yes, Phebe," he answered, "Thar's stirrin' news. The State has seceded. I want to talk over things with Mrs. Hawkins. Won't you come with me?"

"But how can I? I can't leave the children," she answered.

"Take 'em along," he replied, "Mrs. Hawkins will be glad to see them. I'll look after Robby, while you mind the baby. And hurry up. It won't do to keep the little ones out after dark, and I've a good deal to say to Mrs. Hawkins."

In not many minutes the wife was seated upon the horse behind the husband, and though the distance was nearly eight miles over a rough mountain road, in less than two hours the party were climbing the steep path that led up to the dwelling of Mrs. Hawkins. They had no sooner entered the open gateway than a large hound sprang forward to meet them with lively demonstrations of welcome.

The noisy greeting of the dog brought one of the family to the door, and soon the visitors had entered a wide hall, and been ushered into the sitting-room of the spacious log mansion. This apartment, which extended the entire depth of the building, presented a curious mixture of elegance and rusticity. Against a wall of matched boarding, colored a soft gray tint, and ornamented with forest leaves and branches of fern, were hung, in heavy gilt frames, old family portraits, and battle pieces by well-known artists; and on a rough stone-hearth rested a brass fender, and andirons, of rare and antique pattern. A carved table was in the centre of the room, a cushioned sofa against one of the walls, and hair-seated chairs were scattered about in close proximity to others in rustic frames and deer-skin bottoms. The floor was covered with a home-made rag-carpet, and here and there about the apartment was the oval mat of the same material, which was the pride of our great-grand-mothers. Over the door, on a rack of deer's horn, were suspended a couple of long-barreled rifles, and along the farther wall, on plain oak shelves, were perhaps a hundred volumes that would have graced a scholar's library. The trophy of Sukey's encounter with the panther, was spread before the hearth, on which blazed a birch-wood fire, filling the room with a peculiar fragrance, and dis-pelling the chilliness that even late in May clings to the atmosphere in these mountain altitudes.

Before this fire sat Mrs. Hawkins, her rich chestnut hair, not yet streaked with gray, nor her expressive face seamed with the deep lines that tell of a sorrowful his-tory. She gave her visitors a quiet, but cordial greeting, and then, while she lifted the little boy upon her knee, she said, " You bring bad news, Reuben. I see it in your troubled face."

" I do, ma'am," he answered, taking a chair near her, while his wife seated herself beside him. " The country is gone — the State has declared itself out of the Union."

" I've expected it ever since Virginia seceded," she remarked in a quiet tone.

" Tennessee will probably go next, and Kentucky and Maryland will follow; and then we shall have hot-pitch, and standing armies, to our heart's content."

"No doubt we shall — for a time — but the line will be distinctly drawn between slavery and freedom," replied Mrs. Hawkins.

"And we shall be on the wrong side of it, madam, and I want my boys brought up in freedom. I have come to ask you what I shall do — I'm thinking I'd better go back to Ohio."

"What! Will you give up your property, and abandon the post God has given you, at the bidding of traitors? You will not escape the war by doing that, Reuben," she remarked, with decided earnestness.

"Then you think that war will come?"

"I don't see how it can be avoided. Have you not heard of the uprising at the North over the news from Fort Sumter?"

"Yes; and if there is to be war I want to fight on the right side. I will not lift a hand against the country — I'd sooner give up all I have, and go back to Ohio."

"If you stay here, can you not refuse to fight?"

"No, Mrs. Hawkins," he answered, "The Governor has already called for thirty thousand men, and the Legislature has declared every man a traitor who doesn't support North Carolina. If the thirty thousand don't volunteer, they'll be drafted, and forced into the ranks."

"If I were a man," said Mrs. Hawkins, "I think no State could force me to fight against my convictions; and, woman as I am, I believe I can prevent the Confederacy obtaining a single recruit from among these mountains; and you, Reuben Ellis, can help me do it."

"How can I help you, Mrs. Hawkins?" asked Ellis.

8

"By telling these people the truth — that they are asked to fight for a system which keeps them in poverty and ignorance. Slavery does that. It shuts every respectable employment against the poor white man. The fact that all honest work was done by the slave was what forced the fathers of these people to these sterile mountains, and, being here, the slave-holders have legislated for a hundred years to keep them in ignorance. To be convinced that slavery is the cause of all the poverty and ignorance you see, you have only to contrast the condition of the people here with that of the poor white men you have seen in the North. The slave-holders say openly that they secede because the country has elected a President who is unfriendly to slavery; and they mean to erect a new government to make the system perpetual. If the poor white man here understood this, and realized the effect of slavery upon himself, would he fight to uphold it, and fasten it upon his children forever? You, Reuben, have lived in Ohio, and so you know what freedom does for the working man. You can tell this to these people; they trust you, and will believe what you say, for you were born among them."

"I think they would believe me," said Reuben; "but if they did, and should refuse to fight, what would it amount to? The Confederacy would force us into the ranks, for what could we do against the whole South?"

"Do?" exclaimed Mrs. Hawkins, "you could do your duty; you could die right here in your own mountains. Better do that than to fight against the right, and your own freedom. I have three boys that I love better than

I love my life ; but I would see them all dead at my feet
rather than have them lift a hand against their country.
But the Confederacy cannot force you to fight for it.
You can hide among the mountains, and we women will
raise the crops, and supply you with food. If they send
men against you, you can resist them, and if you are
killed in the struggle, it will be better to die so than in
fighting to uphold slavery."

"What you say decides me, Mrs. Hawkins," said Ellis.
"I will stand my ground, and try to do my duty."

"I know you will, Reuben," she answered, "for you
are sound and true to the heart's core. And keep up
good courage; for the end is sure. The right must
triumph. Slavery is about to bring upon itself its own
destruction."

The Governor's call for thirty thousand troops was
promptly responded to by about twenty thousand ; but
no sooner had the first alarm subsided than the general
enthusiasm cooled down, and the people went about their
ordinary pursuits as if the first throes of an earthquake
were not shaking the Continent. This was especially true
of the mountain region. A recruiting station had been
established at Asheville, under Colonel James G. Martin,
but neither his appeals, nor the actual invasion of the
State, and capture of Roanoke Island, by General Burnside, availed to induce the mountain population to tender
their services to the Confederacy. They heard the distant echoes of the war, and the sounds were not unwel-
come, for taught by such hopeful prophets as Reuben

Ellis and Nancy Hawkins, they regarded them as the first foretellings of their own emancipation. "Without the shedding of blood," said Mrs. Hawkins, "there is no remission; and for its great crime of two hundred years, the country must make expiation. The clash of antagonistic principles always precedes national progress, and only through bloody struggle can the country advance to true freedom. The clash has come, and whatever may happen to us, the end is sure, for God reigns."

Cheered by such words, the mountain people of this neighborhood abode at their homes, and it is said, that during the entire year next succeeding the fall of Fort Sumter, not a solitary one of them was enrolled in the ranks of Secession.

The forces of the Confederacy had been so largely reduced by desertion, and the casualties of war, that when the Federal armies began operations in February, 1862, it was wholly unprepared to meet them. In this emergency President Davis called upon the Confederate Congress to resort to a general conscription. The Congress accordingly passed an act on the 16th of April, 1862, which declared all male citizens of the Confederacy, between the ages of eighteen and thirty-five, soldiers during the continuance of the war, or until they should have arrived at the age of thirty-five. Each man was to be allowed thirty days to volunteer; but failing to do so, and not appearing for actual duty, within that time, he was to be regarded as guilty of desertion from the ranks, and liable to its penalty — death at the order of a drum-head court-martial.

When the foregoing action of Congress became known in the mountain region, Reuben Ellis called all the men of the neighborhood together, and they unanimously resolved to resist the conscription. They formed themselves into a company with Ellis as captain, and Alexander Hawkins as lieutenant, and it was decided that every man should go constantly armed in readiness to encounter the conscript officers. A signal system was also agreed upon by which to convey tidings, and call the men together to meet any sudden emergency.

The spirit which animated the community is indicated by the reply of Mrs. Hawkins to her older sons when told by them that they were drafted to fight for the Confederacy. "Fight!" she echoed — "fight against your country, while there are woods you can hide among! I had rather see you dead at my feet! Go! take your guns, and go into the mountains. There is a God in Heaven, and He will see that the right is not finally overcome."

The young men did not go at once into the mountains, and soon an occasion arose which tested their resolution. Services were held regularly in the little log meeting-house, and though Parson Justin was not as zealous as Paul, nor as eloquent, and mighty in the scriptures as Apollos, they were tolerably well attended, for, with the help of Mrs. Hawkins, the Parson did manage to give the people some grains of truth, though it was mixed with the weeds which had sprung up in that section during a century of ignorance. These weeds Mrs. Hawkins could not altogether extirpate, and she was forced to let them grow up with the wheat, trusting that time would winnow them apart.

The church was located where two roads meet, and the building had but one door, and four small windows, protected by solid plank shutters, but at this season left open to admit the refreshing June breezes. On the occasion that is referred to, nearly a hundred persons were in the house, about thirty of whom were men, all with their loaded rifles near at hand — on the floor at their feet, or leaning against the rough benches on which they were seated. Mrs. Hawkins and her three sons were present, occupying benches near the raised platform on which stood the rude pine table which served as the Parson's pulpit.

The Parson had gotten to about his forty-ninth "Ah!" when a young man dressed in gray, entered the house, and coolly helped himself to a draught of water from a pail that stood near the door-way. After thus quenching his thirst, he turned to the Preacher, and said, "Parson, I am sorry to interrupt you; but I have orders to take every man here, who is subject to military duty, to Asheville. If any refuse to go, I have men at hand to compel them."

For a moment all was confusion, but before the sergeant had ceased speaking, Mrs Hawkins had said to her sons, "Resist him, if you have to die for it." At once Alexander sprang to his feet, rifle in hand, and said, "Who are you?"

"An officer of the Government, with orders from Colonel Martin to see that you do your duty," said the sergeant.

"We decline to obey the order," replied Aleck. "Neither Colonel Martin, nor any other man, has a right to enforce such an order on the Sabbath. We shall resist you. Let the women and children pass out — then take us if you can."

The women and children had till this time kept their seats, and either from stolidity, or the cool intrepidity that seems inborn with these people, they had exhibited very little excitement; but the thirty or more men were now all upon their feet with their rifles in their hands. The sergeant glanced around upon the bearded, resolute-looking fellows, and then said, "You outnumber me three to one, I shall not now attempt to enforce my orders; but I shall come again, and then, if you resist, you will wish you hadn't."

"We'll not bandy words with you," replied Aleck. "Now go. I will not answer for your lives, if you are seen within five miles of this place in an hour's time."

Without reply the sergeant left the building, and in a few moments the clatter of a dozen horses' feet was heard receding rapidly along the highway leading to Marshall and Asheville. The men in the church now resumed their seats as if nothing had happened; but after a brief conference with his mother, and before the Parson resumed the services, Aleck said to them, "I think all of you had better go directly to your homes, and arouse your neighbors. This man will keep his word, and if there is an additional force at Marshall, he will be upon us to-night. My brother will ride over at once to notify Captain Ellis, and the rest of you, with as many more as you can muster, had better come to my mother's house by set of sun."

With less than his usual deliberation, Parson Justin now closed the Sunday services, and then the congrega-

tion dispersed to their homes — all but the youngest of
the Hawkins boys, who, mounted on the back of Sam,
was soon speeding down the road to the house of Reuben
Ellis. The only highway leading to it was the one taken
by the conscript officers, so the boy moved forward cautiously, his ears alert to the lightest sound that might
come up the road from the retreating Confederates.
They had all of twenty minutes the start of him, but such
was the fleetness of his horse that he had not ridden five
miles, when, in ascending a long hill, he heard their
measured tramp some distance in advance, and at the
top of the hill descried them, not half a mile away, and
turning into the by-path which led to the dwelling of
Reuben Ellis.

The whole truth flashed at once upon the boy. If
Ellis were at home, he would be inevitably captured.
This came to the lad's mind, and also the fact that he
could give him no warning. A dense forest, encumbered
with undergrowth, through which it was impossible for a
horse to penetrate, lined the upper side of the by-path,
while on the lower side stretched open fields, divided by
high fences, to the very verge of the mountain overlooking the French Broad. By neither route could the boy
reach Ellis before the troop of horsemen, who were then
all of a half-mile in advance of him.

Halting for a few moments in a clump of trees, to let
the Confederates turn a bend in the path, and get out of
sight, he then pressed rapidly forward. Using the same
caution at a second bend, and again at a third, he came to
a fourth, where, for about half a mile, the path followed

an air-line to the dwelling. If he ventured upon this open stretch of pathway before the troop had left it, he would be inevitably seen; but impatient to get on, he reined his horse directly into the forest, and there, leaving him tethered among some undergrowth, he set off on a rapid run through the woods and laurel bushes, reaching a spot about a hundred rods in the rear of the house of Ellis, just as the Confederates had gathered around the entrance, and were preparing to batter down the door with a stout sapling.

This indicated that Ellis was at home, had refused to surrender, and was about to resist the conscript officers. It was one against thirteen, and, fight as bravely as he might, the chances against Ellis were desperate. The lad had with him merely a revolver; had he brought his rifle he might have given the troop a flank-fire; as it was, he could only look on, and see his friend either killed or captured.

Soon he saw half a dozen of the troop bearing the sapling, advance toward the house. When within about twenty paces of the dwelling, they halted, and what seemed to young Hawkins a brief parley, followed. Then the men set forward again, and, an instant later, a shot echoed among the hills, and a man loosened his hold of the sapling, and fell to the ground wounded; then another shot followed and another man fell, and another, and another, in rapid succession, till four of the troop lay upon the ground writhing and cursing.

The Confederates then fell back a few paces, and Ellis ceased firing; but in a moment the sergeant called out to

9

his men, "He has exhausted his fire, come on now, all of you, before he has time to reload." The men sprang to the improvised battering-ram, and rushed with it against the door. Then the boy heard a crash, followed by a few shouts and curses, and then by a dead silence. No shot was fired, so Ellis was doubtless not killed, but captured.

In a few moments young Hawkins observed two men come out of the house, and approach another who had been left in charge of the horses. Then the three led the animals up to the dwelling, and as they approached it the others bore Ellis out upon the lawn bound, and followed by his wife, wringing her hands, and lamenting. Then the men lifted Ellis upon one of the animals, and secured him by a rope tied around his legs, and under and over the body of the horse, and by a leathern strap passed across the breast of a trooper who had mounted in front of him.

While this was being done, others of the troop were attending to the wounded. Three of them were able to sit their horses, the other was evidently dead ; for his body was simply strapped upon the back of a horse, which was led by another of the soldiers. These proceedings occupied perhaps twenty minutes, and then the boy saw the troop move off, and Ellis turn, look back, and speak to his wife, who was following him with agonizing cries and gestures.

As the party passed into the path leading to the highway the lad was for a few moments shielded from their observation, and he improved this time to dart to the barn, from which, without being seen, he could reach the house. There he sat down on a bench before the door, and waited the return of Phebe who, with her little boy, had followed on after the troop, to get a last look at her husband.

Soon she re-appeared at the corner of the house; and springing to his feet, the lad ran to her, saying, "Don't grieve for Reuben, Phebe. He isn't dead; and we'll have him back safe and sound by to-morrow morning. Thar'll be a hundred men at our house by sundown; and we'll rescue Reuben, if we have to burn the whole of Asheville."

"They won't take him to Asheville," said Phebe. "He has right smart of friends thar, and they're afeard of a rescue. I yered them say so."

"Well, no matter whar they take him, we'll have him, *sure*," answered the boy. "Now, let me tell you what to do. I'll saddle your horse, and you get upon him with the baby, and go straight to mother. I'll stay here till I see which way the rascals go, and then, I'll follow with Robby. I've got Sam in the woods close by. Mother'll know what to do, for she has a head like a general. And you tell her I *had* to skulk, or they'd have gobbled me up—but I never wanted a rifle so much in my life."

The distressed woman dried her tears, and making some hasty preparations, was soon on the way to the dwelling of Mrs. Hawkins. Young Hawkins then brought his horse in from the woods, and soon afterward resumed his seat in front of the house, whence he could overlook Marshall, and a long stretch of the highway up and down the French Broad river.

The distance by the road was only five miles, but encumbered as they were with wounded, the troop of horsemen moved slowly, and it was upward of an hour before the boy saw them emerge from the mountain road at the blacksmith's shop, and come to a halt before the hotel at Marshall. There they left their dead and disabled comrades; and when they resumed their route the lad observed that only eight were in the party — one, doubtless, having stayed behind to attend upon the wounded.

Notwithstanding what Phebe had said, the lad expected that Ellis would be taken to Asheville, that being the Confederate head-quarters; he was therefore surprised to see the troop turn squarely about at the hotel; and come directly toward him along the river road, till they reached the bridge which spans the French Broad at the northern end of Marshall. This they crossed, and then, at a rapid gallop, plunged into the ravine which there indents the opposite mountain.

Springing to his feet as the troop passed out of sight, the boy exclaimed, " Well, that is ahead of me! I say, Sam, whar are those fellows going?"

Sam looked up from his browsing on the grass, came directly to his master, and gave a low whinny, but no other answer to the question. If he had any opinion on the subject, he was not far enough advanced in the English language to give it expression.

The lad then locked the cottage door, lifted the little boy, Robby, upon his horse, and in a few moments was fleeing like the wind down the path leading to the high-road. As he reached the summit of the long hill from which he had first seen the Confederates, he looked toward his home, then about five miles away, and there, soaring high upon the air, he beheld a dense column of smoke; and then, casting his eye in other directions, he saw answering columns, in all about a score, rising from among the trees, as if the forests were on fire, every here and there, for a range of twenty miles, along the northern horizon. "Hurrah!" shouted the boy, "Aleck will get two hundred men together. It's not more'n two o'clock, and we'll be on the track of those fellows long before sundown. Come, Sam, show your heels."

In not much more than half an hour the lad rode up the steep path that led to his mother's dwelling. She was seated before the door with Phebe by her side, and near her on the lawn were gathered about thirty men, armed with rifles and revolvers, and holding their horses by the bridles.

The boy had no sooner entered the gateway. than Phebe called out to him, "Which way did they go, Billy?"

"Across the French Broad, and up the road along the Little Pine," answered the lad, springing from his horse, and helping the little boy to the ground.

The announcement was received with exclamations of surprise from all in the assemblage except Mrs. Hawkins and a man standing near her, who from his dress seemed of a better class than the others. He was about thirty years of age, somewhat above the medium height, and of a slight, but erect and muscular frame. His face betokened uncommon intelligence. He had a broad and open forehead, a prominent nose, regular features, and gray eyes, large, deep, and penetrating. In manner he was quiet and unassuming; but he had that air of intense earnestness which indicates in its possessor a purpose worthy of his powers. Though he was much slighter of frame, he bore the resemblance to Reuben Ellis that tells of a common ancestry. They were, in fact, blood relations, but the kinship was so remote that neither of them ever took the trouble to trace it. His home was in Carter county, Tennessee, near the western foot of the Alleghanies, and he had already become widely known as one of the most uncompromising Union men in his State. He had now crossed the mountains to lay in North Carolina the lines of the "underground road," over which he subsequently passed many thousands of escaped prisoners, and loyal fugitives, to the Union lines. He was the Daniel Ellis, whose exploits are familiar to every one at all acquainted with the war in the South-west.

When the others had spoken, Mrs. Hawkins turning to Ellis, said, "Please give us your opinion, Mr. Ellis."

"Let me ask you a question or two," he answered. "Is there a road that way to Asheville? and what is the feeling of the people beyond the French Broad?"

"A road branches off to Asheville at the Sandy Mush, about ten miles back of Marshall," she replied. "The people over there, I have heard, are generally in favor of the Union; though there is a nest of Rebels in Swain county, where they have a very strong jail called 'the Black-Hole of Charleston.'"

"Then, madam, they have either gone that way to Asheville," said Ellis, "or they are taking him to the

Black-Hole at Charleston. We can tell which at the Sandy Mush crossing. My advice would be that the men now here set out at once, without waiting for any more, in order to be at the Sandy Mush before nightfall. I am familiar with this kind of business, and I will go with the men if you do not object — my principal purpose in coming here was to meet Reuben."

"If you take command, Mr. Ellis," said Mrs. Hawkins, "I feel sure Reuben will be rescued."

All the men expressed approval, and quickly bounded into their saddles, and among the others the youngest son of Mrs. Hawkins. Observing this his mother said to him, "I think you'd better not go Billy, Sam has traveled fifteen miles to-day, and will break down."

"No, he won't, mother," answered the boy. "He's good for another hundred miles, and I wouldn't be left behind for all of Madison county."

CHAPTER IV.

THE RESCUE OF ELLIS.

On crossing the bridge at Marshall, the rescuing party found the trail of the eight horsemen deeply imprinted in the sand along the river bank. This trail they followed through a dense forest, and up a steep and stony road, for a distance of about three miles, when they came to Little Pine creek, where they halted to allow their horses a draught of the clear, ice-cold mountain water. Resuming then their way they followed the road along the Little Pine till they reached its source on the summit of the mountain, near an abandoned dwelling. Here all trace of a highway disappeared, and nothing was to be seen except an open field, now lying waste, but showing signs of recent cultivation. But right across that open field, and down the long incline which there slopes gently to the Sandy Mush, were the tracks of the eight horsemen.

Encouraged by these fresh signs, the party pressed rapidly on down the mountain, and fully three hours before sunset, came to the Sandy Mush, the tracks of the eight horsemen still before them, but headed direct for Asheville. They pressed on again, fearful that the prey had escaped them, but determined to follow to the very jail of Buncombe county, if their way should not be barred by greatly superior numbers. Another two miles brought them to Turkey creek, a branch of the Sandy Mush, and flowing into it not far from the French Broad, and here, to their inexpressible relief, they saw that the horsemen had left the high road, and taken up a narrow path along the creek, and over the Turkey Mountain.

One of the party had been that way on a hunting excursion, and he thought that at the distance of about ten miles they would strike the Waynesville road, near the bridge over "Forks of Pigeon" and about fifteen miles from Asheville. To avoid intelligence of their movements reaching the Confederate head-quarters, it was desirable that they should not reach the high-road before dark, but they pushed on as rapidly as the rugged nature of the ground would permit, and not far from "an hour by sun" had crossed the aforesaid bridge at the distance of about three miles west of the hamlet of Hominy.

Until this time the tracks of the horsemen had been plainly before them, but now, blended as they were with the many foot-prints of the highway, they were no longer a safe guide to follow. The troop had halted at the west end of the bridge, when "Billy-Boy," who, because it was impossible for him, or his horse, to keep still, had ridden about half a mile up the road, came thundering back, saying, "Thar's an old fellow camped out up thar in the trees, who I reckon can tell us all we want to know. I didn't question him for fear I should make a blunder."

Leaving the body of mountaineers at the bridge, Ellis and Aleck Hawkins rode forward with the boy, and soon came upon a company of travelers who had gone into

10

camp in a·grove by the roadside. There were nine in the party, all in the lowest stage of forlornness. The father of the family had unkempt gray hair, a deeply-wrinkled face, and appeared to be nearly seventy years of age. His only clothing was a battered hat, a coarse, soiled shirt, and a pair of trousers so covered with patches as to have lost all vestige of the original fabric. Two young men, evidently his sons, were even more ragged than he, and in addition were bare-footed and with legs naked half-way to the knees. The wife, who was all of twenty years younger than the husband, had no other clothing than a cotton sun-bonnet, and a greasy linsey gown. A full-grown daughter was attired in a similar manner. The other children were also bare-footed, and even more ragged than their brothers, and their only head-covering was a mass of tangled, yellowish hair. All had stolid faces, and a woe-begone, spiritless look, which betokened no aspiration in life beyond the mere satisfaction of the animal appetites. A bundle of tattered blankets lay near them on the grass, and scattered about were an iron kettle, a dilapidated coffee-pot, a half-consumed ham, and a bag of corn-meal. In the hollow of a tree the eldest daughter was building a fire, with the evident intention of preparing their supper, and for this repast the remainder of the family were idly waiting, seated, or stretched at full length, upon the ground.

As Ellis halted before these "low down" people the old man rose to his feet, and saluted him with the usual "How d'ye." To this Ellis civilly responded, adding, "Where are you traveling?"

"We uns is from ahind uv Asheville, an' bound fur the Smokies. Reckon we kin light on a few acres thar as doan't b'long ter nobody."

"But it's a poor country — why do you leave a better region?"

"Ter git rid uv this cussed war — but I reckon hit has got thar afore us, fur they toted a pore feller along yere not more'n two hours agone, bound hand and foot. He'd tried ter dodge the conscription."

"I reckon the only way to dodge it is to get through to the Union lines," said Ellis, "so you'd better have staid where you were, unless you have friends in this section."

"We uns hain't no friends, nowhar — doan't know nobody, 'cept hit mont be Squire Barnet, ez keeps bait fer man and beast ter Waynesville. Reckon he'll d'rect we uns whar ter gwo, fur he'm a right decent man."

"What is Barnet's full name?" asked Ellis.

"Jeems — from t'other side uv the Unakas — over ter Tennessee."

Then, with a kindly "good evening" to the old man, Ellis and his two companions rode slowly up the road. When out of hearing of the corn-cracker, Ellis said to Aleck Hawkins, "I knew Barnet fifteen years ago, and I am greatly mistaken if he is not a loyal man. I think we had better talk with him; and I would suggest that your brother should ride back, and tell the men to follow us slowly, and on no account to enter Waynesville till they hear from us."

Ellis and Aleck Hawkins rode forward at a brisk pace, and at the distance of about seven miles, entered the

town of Waynesville. The town is now a summer resort of considerable celebrity, having two broad parallel
streets, lined with brick or newly-painted wooden dwellings, and an imposing brick court-house. At this period,
however, it was unknown to fame, and consisted almost
entirely of a dilapidated temple of justice, with dingy
walls, a tan-bark floor, and battered windows; together
with a half dozen log and frame rookeries, and the two-
storied public house kept by James Barnet. Such extreme caution would seem to have been unnecessary in
approaching a place of so little importance, but Ellis
knew it to be court-week, and expected to find the town
crowded with a thousand people, the most of the men
carrying arms, after the universal custom of the
country.

The sun had been down nearly an hour, and after the
short twilight of this mountain region, the night had
come on without moon or star, and in deep darkness;
but as they entered the town a blaze of light shone from
two rows of canvas-covered wagons that lined the sides
of the grass-grown street, and the hotel was illuminated
at nearly every one of its windows. Ellis wedged his
way, with young Hawkins, through the throng about the
hotel, into the hall of the building, and then asked a servant to bring to him the landlord. A middle-aged, respectable person soon appeared, and Ellis inquired of him
for lodgings for himself and friend. "It's an impossible
thing, Sir," replied Mr. Barnet. "My house is full to
overflowing." Then, as a sudden gleam lit up his face,
he added, extending his hand, "Why, How d'ye! I

didn't at first know you. My house *is* full, but I'll stow you two away if I have to give up my own bedroom. Step this way, if you please;" and he led the way to a room in a remote part of the house, leaving the crowd of bystanders to wonder who the strangers were to whom he was showing such unusual attention.

When they had entered his apartment, and he had carefully closed the door, he turned to Ellis, saying, " Daniel Ellis, this is foolhardy. If you were known to be here, you'd be strung to a tree in half an hour."

"Then you know me?" said Ellis, in a quiet tone.

"I do, though you couldn't have been more than fifteen when I left Carter county. Is this gentleman from Tennessee?"

"No! said Ellis, "He is a son of Mrs. Hawkins of Madison county."

"Indeed!" exclaimed Mr. Barnet, "I've heard of Mrs. Hawkins. I am proud to have you under my roof, Sir. And I'm proud, too, to have you, Daniel, for I've heard all about your doings."

"Then you are a loyal man," said Ellis, "I felt sure that you were."

"I am a loyal man; but I have to use policy, particularly with such a crowd as is here to-night. All the Charleston roughs are in town, and will be as long as Court is in session."

"That suits us exactly," said Ellis. "Are there many loyal men around here?"

"A good many lying out in the woods. I wish you could get them through the lines."

"I can and will. They've only to report to me or Treadaway at Elizabethton."

Ellis then disclosed to Mr. Barnet the object of his visit, and the latter informed him that the men who had captured Reuben Ellis had stopped at his house for supper, and were conveying him to the Black-Hole at Charleston, where it was expected he would be tried, and executed on the following day. He had no chance for mercy, for he had killed a soldier who was doing his duty. He furthermore told him that it would be nothing short of madness for the squad of thirty horsemen to attempt to pass through Waynesville. They might get through without opposition, but they would be seen, their errand suspected, and the entire country raised about their ears before they got to Charleston. The only safe course was to pass around the place. There was no road, but he had a trusty negro whom he would send to guide them through the woods, and open-fields, to a point where they could again take the highway.

The negro having been brought into the room, that he might know Mr. Ellis, the landlord accompanied his guests to the front-entrance, where, as he parted from them, he said in a tone loud enough to be heard by the bystanders, "I am very sorry I can't give you lodgings for the night, Mr. Jones; but you will be sure of good quarters at the Squire's — remember it is the third house on the right, beyond the village." Then remounting their horses, the two rode leisurely down the road to the encampment of the mountaineers.

The moon was casting a dim light over the dense forest that lined the highway, when the old negro halted in the road about half a mile east of the village, and uttering a faint whistle, said, "Am you dar, Massa Jones?"

"We are here," was the response, as Ellis and "Billy-Boy" emerged upon their horses from among the trees. "You are late — has any thing happened?"

"Nuffin', Massa, only Zeke had to see Squar Plotts, an' him wasn't ter home. You uns neber'd git fru widout him."

"Why not without him?" inquired Ellis.

"Case he'll hab ter show you uns; fur de road am nigh all the way fru him grounds."

"Can he be trusted?"

"Trusted, Massa! Why, nigh on fifty year ago he buy Zeke, and guv him his freedom, when Zeke he was so sick an' nigh ter death, dat he wouldn't fotch more'n two hundred dollar; and all dat time Massa Plotts hab led de class in de meetin!"

"All the saints and class-leaders are not loyal men," said Ellis, "but, Uncle, I'll trust *you*; I'd stake my life on you twice a week. Now, which way do we go — this or the other side of the road?"

"Dis side, Massa — de Squar lib 'bout half a mile back."

"Then it's the house near where the men are encamped. Jump up behind me, Uncle, and we'll be there in a few minutes."

The mountaineers were in readiness, and moving slowly through the forest, they soon came to a halt in a woods about a hundred rods in the rear of a two-storied log dwelling standing in the midst of a treeless clearing. Here, the black, putting his hand to his mouth, gave a peculiar whistle, and instantly a horseman emerged from the shadow of the house, and rode toward them. As he came near, Ellis saw by the dim moonlight that he wore a long white beard, was much bent with age, and dressed in the usual homespun, with a slouched hat of expansive dimensions. He was the first to speak. When well within the shadow of the trees he said to Aleck Hawkins, who sat his horse by the side of Ellis, "I'm proud to meet ye, Mr. Hawkins. I know'd yer father. We didn't think exactly alike, but he war a right good man, and he gave me much edification."

"I am glad to meet any one who thought well of my father," answered young Hawkins, "and the more glad to meet you, Sir, if you get us around this difficulty."

"I shall be pleased to do it, Sir," replied the old man, "and it's easy done. All ye hev ter do is ter observe a dead silence while we is passin' near the house'n. But yer are on a desperate tramp; and if thar was ary other way to save Reuben Ellis, I'd advise ye ter turn round, and git back ter yer homes as soon as ye kin."

"There is no other way, Sir," said young Hawkins, "and Reuben's life is worth more than any of ours, except this gentleman's, Mr. —— Jones."

"Yes," responded the old man, reaching out his hand, and grasping that of Ellis, "Zekiel told me ye had done a heap for the Union, over thar ter Tennessee. Ye mout know him they call Dan Ellis."

"Oh, yes! I know him," said Ellis. "I slept under the same tree with him not more than a week ago."

"Well, he's a true man. I hope he'll be preserved to do much for his kentry. I would loike ter take him by the hand, and tell him what I think of him. But come, we'd better be movin'."

In single file, and profound silence, the troop then threaded its way through the dense forest, and the fence-less corn-fields, till at the close of about an hour they struck the highway at a point something more than four miles west of Waynesville. There the old man halted his horse at the margin of the road, and said to Ellis, "Now the way is clar' afore ye, hit's a long thirty mile, but with sech critters as yours ye ought ter make it in good time. I've never been inside the prison; but ye know its reckoned the strongest in Car'lina. Ye'll need ter know the lay uv the land fore ye attempt ter break inter it, and I'm thinkin' ye'd better stop ter th' first white house out uv Charleston,— the only painted one round thar — and tell yer business to Squar Staley; ye kin depend on him. I'd gwo on with ye myself, but I can't very well stand this night ridin'. I fit all through the Mexican war, but now I'm too old to be uv ary more sarvice ter my kintry."

"You're not too old to be of great service to us, Mr. Plotts," said Ellis. "You are a true man, Sir, and seeing that you think well of me, I'll tell you that I am Dan Ellis."

"Dan Ellis!" echoed the old man, reining his horse nearer to that of Ellis, and scanning his features as closely as he could in the dim moonlight. "Can it be possible?

11

If I'd observed ye afore, I'd a knowed ye was no common
man. It does me proud ter hev sarved ye, Mr. Ellis, and
I'll sarve ye more — I'll gwo along with ye, and we'll hev
Reuben Ellis out, or die a tryin'."

No remonstrance availing to turn the old man from
this purpose, the party set out on a rapid gallop with him,
Ellis and Aleck Hawkins as a vanguard. They passed
the town of Webster, and several farm dwellings on the
way, but encountered not a single human being till, at
about four o'clock in the morning, they drew rein in the
court-yard of Squire Staley, on the outskirts of Charleston. Before the troop had all come up the advance-
guard were seated in the "best-room" of that gentleman,
discussing with him the situation.

The jail, Mr. Staley said, was on the lower floor of the
old court-house. The "Black-Hole," where Reuben Ellis
was confined, was a log-room built within another log-
room, the space between the two being filled with large
stones. It could be entered only by a ladder from a
trap-door in the floor above, and had no other light than
that which could filter itself through the two log walls,
the stone filling-in, and the decayed outside weather-
boarding. The trap-door was secured by a padlock, the
key of which was kept by the jailer — a morose, ferocious
fellow, who lived alone in the jail, and seldom left it by
day or by night. His apartments adjoined the "Black-
Hole," and in his sleeping-room was a narrow iron-barred
opening communicating with it, through which he could
watch a prisoner. The only way to rescue Ellis was to
secure the jailer, and get the key of the padlock from

him, and this would have to be done without noise, for the least disturbance might alarm the eight soldiers, who slept not two hundred feet away, and also arouse the whole town. The jailer was always well-armed, and, to avoid bloodshed, must be taken unawares; but Mr. Staley thought he slept with his door unlocked, as did every one else in the vicinity. However, he would himself go along to ascertain that fact, and if it should not be so, some pretext must be invented to draw the jailer to the door, when they could seize and gag him without difficulty. A trusty Indian, named Hocus, who lived with Mr. Staley, might help them in this emergency; but the affair must be managed so as not to implicate the Indian in it, or it might cost him his life.

At this point Mr. Staley left the room, and soon returned with the Indian, Hocus. He was a full-blooded Cherokee, born and reared among these mountains, which had been the home of his nation for untold centuries. He wore the ordinary homespun of the district, cut in the usual fashion, and there was nothing peculiar about him except his moccasins, and an eye of striking keenness and brilliancy. He listened attentively to Mr. Staley's statement of what might be required of him, and then said, "The door will not be locked; I will guide the gentlemen to where he sleeps — the rest they'll have to be quick about, or he'll kill some of them."

As they moved slowly along the one street of the town, at whose farther end stood the old court-house, Ellis and Alexander Hawkins arranged the details of the enterprise. They and four of the coolest and most powerful of the men, were to enter the building guided by the Cherokee; twelve of the others were to surround the house where the soldiers were lodged, and the remainder of the troop, dismounted, were to station themselves in front of the jail, ready for whatever emergency might arise. Mr. Staley and Mr. Plotts were to be inactive spectators, from some point where they would not, if seen, be suspected of complicity in the rescue. When all was in readiness, it lacked less than an hour of day-break.

The Cherokee found the outer door unlocked, and, noiselessly entering the building, he soon returned, saying to Ellis, "I've left his door open. He is asleep, a light burning. Take off your boots, and be quick about the business."

The Indian guided them to the jailer's door, and noiselessly the six men entered a room about twelve feet square, which by the dim light of a lantern standing upon the hearth, they saw was somewhat the filthiest apartment ever tenanted by a human being. The floor was littered over with broken bottles, worn-out saddles, bits of harness, and a dilapidated rocking-chair. On the wall was an array of shackles, in one corner a huge packing-box, made to do duty as a desk, and in the other, a low, tattered bed, the bedstead manufactured from old joist and clapboards, which had been torn from some dismantled dwelling. Reclining on one end of this bed was a pair of huge boots, on the other an enormous beard, surmounted by heavy black brows, beneath which were a pair of closed eyes. In the duskiness of the room the man's other features could not be distinguished. He lay absolutely motionless, and was evidently sleeping soundly.

Taking all this in at a glance, Ellis looked at young Hawkins, put one hand upon his mouth, and with the other pointed to the iron bracelets; and then, before the jailer was fully awake, he was securely gagged, and bound hand and foot with his own manacles. All this was done without a word being spoken. Then young Hawkins thrust his hand into the prostrate man's pocket, and drew out three keys, one large and two smaller ones, and holding them up to Ellis, exclaimed, "Here they are! The Lord be thanked. We'll have Reuben free in five minutes." As he said this a voice from behind the iron grating, over the packing-box, asked, "Is that you, Aleck?"

"It is, Reuben," he answered; "and in my hand are the keys of your shackles, and the dungeon."

All now left the jailer's room, Ellis carefully locking the door, and taking the key with him; and it was not many minutes before Reuben Ellis was at liberty.

CHAPTER V.

THROUGH THE MOUNTAINS.

It wanted still half an hour of daybreak when the troop passed quietly down the village street, and came to a halt in a clump of trees near the dwelling of Squire Staley. As they did so, the Squire and Mr. Plotts approached Reuben Ellis, where he sat astride of Sam, behind the younger Hawkins. The former said to him, "I congratulate you upon your escape, Mr. Ellis; but you are not yet out of danger. It won't do to return by the way of Waynesville. My advice would be that you take the road up the Oconolufta, and through the Cherokee country. Hocus here, can guide you as far as the Big Pigeon."

Ellis thanked him for the suggestion, and then Mr. Plotts remarked, "Ye'll need a horse, Mr. Ellis; take mine, he's a good roadster. If ye kin send him back, very well; if ye can't, count him as so much good-will I bear ter ye."

"But how will you get home, Sir?" asked Reuben. "They tell me you live at Waynesville."

"Oh, I'll loan him a nag," said Mr. Staley. "But we are wasting time. You ought to be on the Oconolufta before any are passing on this road. Here, Hocus, jump on my horse, and guide these folks through your country."

Hurried farewells were then spoken, and then the horsemen set off at a brisk gallop down the road to Waynesville, until they came opposite the point where the Oconolufta joins the Tuckasege. There in Indian file, each horseman treading as nearly as possible in the tracks of the one preceding him—they forded the Tuckasege, and striking a north-east course entered, at the distance of a few miles, the wooded ravine bordered by steep mountain ranges, a mile or more in height, through which flows the picturesque Oconolufta.

They were now in a magnificent region of mighty woods, majestic mountains, and noisy cascades, which leap over precipitous cliffs, and rush in sheeted foam down steep declivities. Here and there a grassy cove indents the side of the ravine, or a quiet, tree-sprinkled valley, where the mountains had receded farther from the river, and left some luxuriant nook to be one day the abode of man. As yet, however, no human habitation can be found in all the forest-covered region, and a stillness unbroken save by the noisy rush of the river, the startled cry of some bird, or the occasional bleat of a deer, or growl of a bear, reigns over all the leafy solitude. The air was fresh and exhilarating, the sky cloudless and serene, and the men journeyed on with light hearts, elated with the successful issue of their enterprise, and careless of any danger that might be awaiting them.

The sun had been up for an hour when the cavalcade entered this secluded thoroughfare, but it was a longer time before its slant beams penetrated to the recesses of the ravine, and dissipated the keen chill that always loads the early morning air in these high mountain altitudes. Then the tired men went into camp to rest from their fatigue, and to refresh their jaded animals, which now had been upon the march for upward of eighty miles, with only the brief halting-time they had caught at Waynesville and Charleston.

On first entering the ravine the men had shot a couple of deer without so much as leaving their saddles, and from these, and the parched corn-meal which each one carried at his saddle-bow, they soon prepared a bountiful breakfast. This partaken of, they stretched themselves upon the thick green grass, on which their animals were browsing, and sank into a slumber that lasted till long after midday. This was true of every one of the troop except the three leaders, and two of the men, who had been sent up and down the road to give warning of the approach of any hostile party.

But the approach of an enemy was not anticipated. The presence of the mountaineers was doubtless still unknown at Waynesville, and their entrance and departure from Charleston had probably not been seen or heard by one of its inhabitants; and such were the hermit-like habits of the jailer, as reported by the Cherokee, Hocus, that they concluded the fellow might pass a day or two in fasting and seclusion before his non-appearance among his neighbors would be remarked upon. The danger to the troop they imagined to be from altogether another quarter,— from some strong party of Confederates who might be even then lying in wait for their return at the crossing of the French Broad at Marshall. This contingency they decided to avoid by a flank march down the Big Pigeon, and across the Newfound Mountains to Warm Springs, and thence east to their homes in Madison county.

It was some hours after noon when the tired mountaineers aroused themselves from sleep, prepared a hasty meal, and resumed their journey. Their way was still along the picturesque Oconolufta, the road following the windings of the stream, and in places wedged so closely between the river and the overhanging cliffs as to scarcely allow of the passage of a wheeled vehicle. At the distance of about ten miles from the mouth of the river, they came suddenly upon a broad, open valley in which were evidences of civilization in log farm-houses, fruit orchards, patches of corn, and small herds of the diminutive horse that is styled the "Indian pony." They had entered the Cherokee country — a tract of about fifty thousand acres — all that is left of an immense domain which once comprised nearly the whole of the present States of Tennessee and Kentucky. About one thousand of the tribe are settled here, the original home of their nation. Their fields seemed worn out by injudicious farming; but the general aspect of the country was quite equal to that of the districts occupied by the whites, and the people seen along the road appeared to be as far advanced in civilization. They were dressed in a similar manner, and, except by their moccasins and darker complexions, could not have been distinguished from their

12

Anglo-Saxon neighbors. They were in fact better educated than the whites, for they had free-schools, supported
by the nation.

The road the mountaineers were pursuing runs nearly
parallel to the Waynesville highway till, about three
miles from that town, it strikes the valley of the Big
Pigeon, where it joins the old stage road which, following the windings of the river, goes on to Knoxville. The
troop had journeyed slowly, to further recruit their jaded
horses, and it was after dark when they reached the junc-
tion of the two roads, and looked down upon the town of
Waynesville. As they did so they observed, at a short
distance away, a bright fire blazing among the trees.

The light revealed the long canvas-covered wagon
peculiar to the region, and a party of campers-out, seated
on the ground, and partaking of their supper. As the
troop came nearer, Reuben counted five in the company—
a middle-aged man and woman, and three young men,
the oldest about twenty, all decently clad, and of the
better class of mountain people. He recognized them at
once as a family that had lived about a dozen miles from
his home, on the upper waters of Flat Creek, in Buncombe
county, and approaching them with Dan Ellis he accosted
the older man of the party. "Is that you, Mr. Robbins?"
he said; "moving to your farm on the Pigeon?"

The man looked up, then sprang to his feet, exclaim-
ing, "Reuben Ellis! What'r ye doin' yere? Why,
doan't ye know they is scourin' the hull kentry for ye —
more'n fifty on 'em, armed ter the teeth, an' determined
ter shoot ye down the minit they set eyes on ye?"

"I didn't know it," answered Reuben. "How do you know it?"

"Why, ye see, we uns camped out last night ter Waynesville, and just as we was settin' off for the Pigeon about ten this morning, the sodgers as took ye come thunderin' inter the town, sayin' as half a dozen men had broke inter the jail over night, clapped the padlocks on ter the jailer, and toted ye off scot-free. There was a great rumpus ter onc't, an' in a mazin' quick time, a big squad got together ter the hotel, all armed and mounted, an' most uv 'em the ugliest-lookin' chaps ye ever seed, from round Charleston. I took an intrist in hit, 'case, Reuben, I allers took ter ye, so, I hung round ter see the end on hit. They 'cluded thar war'nt only six or eight on ye, and ye had took some of the by-roads — most likely the one along the Oconolufta — but they'd scour 'em all. So, they goed off in four squads, and I staid by till the last comed back. Then I felt glad ter know they hadn't kotched ye. The squad as come up the road ye is on, said they rid as fur as the Injun town, Yaller Hill, and never come away till two o'clock; but nobody had seed hide or hair uv ye."

"Well," said Reuben, "if they had gone about two miles further along this road, they would have found us, camped out to rest our horses. It was lucky they didn't, for not one of them would have got away to tell the story. What next do they mean to do?"

"They was discussin' that when we uns comed away. The most uv 'em reckon ye're tuck ter the mountings, and ar' makin' yer way ter Tennessee; so, they count

hit'll be time lost to scour the woods, and they'd better
tuck all thar men, and make a stret line down the Big
Pigeon, to head ye off on t'other side of the Smokies. I
reckon they'll do that, and I've been lucking ter see 'em
gwo by every minit since we camped out yere. If ye
doan't want ter fight, I'd advise ye ter put right down
the road, and tuck the first crossin' over the mountings
ter the French Broad. One thing ar sartain — they won't
luck for ye in Madison county — they'll reckon ye won't
dar' ter gwo thar. 'My boys wud gwo along ter holp ye
in case ye has a fight; but ye see we uns hain't nary
critters but one horse an' a mule. But we're on your
side, Reuben. We is movin' ter Pigeon ter be nigher
the woods in case the conscript crowd come fur the
boys."

There was wisdom in the old man's advice, and the
troop acted upon it, setting off at once at a rapid pace
down the road they had intended to travel, the three
leaders keeping about a fourth of a mile in the rear, to
be the first to hear the approach of the expected body of
horsemen.

They passed numerous dwellings — for they were in a
thickly-settled farming region — but encountered no way-
farers, except such as were passing from one house to
another. Continuing their rapid pace till about an hour
before midnight, they came to Fine's Creek, along which
a bridle-path leads up and over the Sandy Mush Mountain, to the high-road on which they had, in coming out,
followed the soldiers. The head of the cavalcade had
turned into the bridle-path when " Billy-Boy," who rode

with the advance, came racing back to the three leaders, saying, " Thar's at least twenty men with torches standing around a house on the shelf of the mountain, about a quarter of a mile from the road. I've halted the troop till you could come up."

In a very few minutes the leaders were with the advance at the foot of the bridle-path, inspecting the suspicious gathering. While they did so the torches disappeared, and a blaze of light streamed down from the open door and windows of the dwelling. " Why, Billy-Boy," said Reuben, " it's only a ' surprise shindy.' There's no danger in that; besides, all these folks are friendly to me. So, lead the men up the path. I'll go to the house and see these people."

The young folks of the neighborhood had descended unawares upon a neighbor to have a midnight dance at his dwelling. When Ellis arrived at the door he saw, by the light of the pine-knots that were blazing on the hearth, some twenty young men and women, all dressed in their best garments, clearing a room of about twenty-five feet square, in preparation for a "shindy," while the master and mistress, just aroused from sleep, were finishing their toilets in a corner. Two of the young fellows were already seated before the fire, tuning a home-made banjo, and an old violin, when, removing his hat, Ellis stepped into the apartment.

For some minutes there was much the same sensation as if a ghost had appeared among them; but when they realized that Ellis was actually flesh and blood, their joy knew no bounds — the women throwing their arms about his neck, the men seizing him by the hand, or arm, or any part of the person that could be shaken. They had heard he had been captured and hanged, and he was to them as one risen from the dead. " Well," he said to them, as soon as the young women allowed him the use of his organs of speech — " it's rather pleasant to come near hanging, for in that way a man finds out he has some friends. Now, good folks, let me say that it is too dark to cross the mountain, and I and my friends propose to camp out on the bench above this. We suppose we are followed by a party from Waynesville, and I want you to know nothing about us, if they happen to inquire when they go by on the road."

This all promised, and then Ellis joined the troop, which soon afterward went into camp, on a shelf of the mountain covered with trees, about a quarter of a mile in the rear of the dwelling. The men ate their suppers without their accustomed bowl of coffee, no fire being built lest it should betray the encampment. This done, they stretched themselves upon the ground, and were soon in deep slumber.

Meanwhile, the leaders held a consultation. The question was, what course to pursue in case the Charleston roughs should pass along the road? Should they be attacked, or allowed to go by unmolested? Daniel Ellis was in favor of attack — he never allowed a Confederate to come within reach of his carbine without giving him some of its contents. Reuben Ellis evidently sympathized with this feeling; but he merely said it would be against the wishes of Mrs. Hawkins. She thought it wrong to take human life except in self-defense.

"We will respect her wishes," replied Dan Ellis. "But hark! there they are — several miles up the river."

Faint it was that distant tread, but measured and musical as the beat of a morning drum heard across leagues of silence. There was no mistaking it — nothing in the forest could create such sounds save only the tramp of a body of horsemen. After listening a few moments, Daniel Ellis said to Aleck, "Would it not be well to rouse the men and have them ready? If you will stay by them, Reuben and I will go down as far as the house to reconnoitre."

As the two reached the corner of the dwelling one of the countrymen stood at the door, listening to the approaching horsemen, and Dan Ellis said to him, "How far away are those men, and how many are there of them?"

"I should guess about twenty-five," answered the man, "and they mout be a mile away."

"Well, I'd sooner trust my ears than yours, young man," said Ellis. "There are at least sixty, and they are two miles away; but coming at a gait that shows they have heard we are on the road. I would give a small farm to try Old Blazer upon them."

"So would I," answered Reuben; "but I wouldn't for a good many farms go against the wishes of Mrs. Hawkins."

Some ten minutes elapsed during which the dance went on, but the men stood listening silently to the rapidly approaching horsemen. Soon the troop emerged into sight — all of sixty, their arms gleaming in the moonlight. In a few moments more they came to a halt in the road at the foot of the bridle-path.

Then, Dan Ellis remarked, "A half-dozen are dismounting; they are coming here to make inquiry. My friend, won't you change your coat and hat with me for a little time? I want to have a talk with these fellows."

The exchange of garments was quickly made, when Ellis said, "Now, my friend, you'd better get into the bushes with Reuben. The Rebels don't like the color of my coat, and they'll nab you if they see you in it." Saying this he passed quietly into the house, and, taking a stand near the door, looked on at the dancers.

It was but a few minutes before the sergeant who had captured Reuben, appeared with a half-dozen other armed men, at the door-way. The dancing suddenly ceased as the sergeant entered the room, and bowing respectfully to the assemblage, said, "I am sorry to disturb you, my friends — but I want to ask if you have seen a number of men on horseback pass down the road within an hour or two?"

"Yas, Cunnel," answered Ellis. "They stopped yere all uv ten minnits."

"Stopped here! What for?" asked the sergeant.

"Ter kiss the gals, I reckon. Leastwise thar wasn't one in the room as Rube Ellis didn't buss, loike as if she was his sweetheart; an' the gals tuck hit as if they rather loiked hit."

This remark was greeted by a suppressed titter from the young women; but the sergeant was in no mood to be amused. He said sharply, "Why! didn't you know he was under arrest for murder and treason?"

" Yas, Cunnel, we uns knowed he'd laid some ten or a dozen on ye out cold, and that ye wus meanin' ter hang him ; but we uns reckoned 'twant just safe ter handle him with Dan Ellis, an' his sixteen-shooter, at his back."

" Dan Ellis ! " exclaimed the sergeant. " Was he with him ? "

" Sartin ; and Rube say hit war Dan as broke inter the jail, and let him loose. Now, if you uns cud kotch Dan t'wud be suthin loike, fur thar's five thousand dollars onter his head."

" How many men had they with them ? " asked the sergeant.

" I'd buy 'em quick fur twenty, ef they was niggers, an' I was in thet business — which I hain't."

" How long is it since they left here ? "

" Hit mout be a hour. They didn't 'pear ter be in no sort uv a hurry. I reckon they'd hev stayed all night if we'd axed 'em."

" Well, my friend," said the sergeant, turning to go, " I'm obliged to you. I'll have those men before morning."

" Take my advice, Cunnel," added Ellis, " hev yer eyes peeled when ye come onter 'em; fur ye knows, Dan has that sixteen-shooter allers handy, an' Rube 'll fight loike blazes when ye git him inter a corner — I reckon ye knows that."

No further incident that needs mention occurred to the fugitives till their arrival, at sunset on the following day, at Warm Springs. There they parted with Daniel Ellis. The remainder of the party, taking the road up the Laurel river, were at Mrs. Hawkins' house by midnight.

13

CHAPTER VI.

CLOSE ESPIONAGE.

On arriving at his home Reuben Ellis found that every hamlet, and every highway and by-way in Madison county, was alive with conscript officers, seeking to force into the Confederate ranks an unwilling population. Colonel Martin was applying himself to this work with a zeal which showed that he was bent upon achieving promotion, if not glory. He was probably familiar with the adage, " You can lead a horse to water, but you cannot make him drink," which saying, applied to military matters, might be rendered, " You can force an unwilling recruit into the ranks, but he will desert at the first opportunity." But this was no concern of his. His business was to furnish the men, not to lead them into battle; and he pursued this work with an unflagging energy which speedily won for him the rank of brigadier-general.

The man to whom Martin intrusted the enforcement of the conscription in Madison county was a Colonel James Keith, one of those miscreants who are thrown to the surface by civil commotions, and are found among all races, and in all latitudes. Keith had himself entered the district the day following the capture of Reuben Ellis, and had the rescuing party made their return by the way of Marshall, they would have found him, with two hundred men, patiently awaiting them at the bridge over the French Broad river.

But Keith no sooner learned that Ellis had taken the road to Tennessee, than he pressed on into the heart of the mountains. Divided into small squads, his men swarmed over the entire country, exploring every woods, and invading every dwelling, but everywhere finding the houses deserted of nearly all except their female occupants. In a single day an extensive region had been converted into a community of old men, women, and children. Every male between the ages of eighteen and thirty-five had suddenly disappeared, and the conscript officers neither saw, nor heard, any thing of them, except the occasional hoot of an owl, cry of a hawk, or bleat of a sheep, issuing from some clump of laurel bushes as they rode along the highways.

Mrs. Glass's receipt for cooking a hare is, "first catch the hare;" but how could these hares be caught when they were fleet of foot, and familiar with every hiding place in the mountains? It could not be done in any trial of speed; it must be effected by stratagem, and therein lay Keith's merit as a military-man. Up to his entering the valley of the Shelton Laurel he had not secured a solitary conscript, but by the time he had arrived in that secluded neighborhood, he had matured a scheme which might, had his word been taken, have speedily secured him an entire regiment.

This valley was less than five miles north of the residence of Mrs. Hawkins, and it contained between eighty and a hundred voters, all attached to the Union, and unwilling to bear arms for the Confederacy. Keith had no sooner entered it than he sent messages to the outlying citizens, assuring them that if they would give up their arms, and submit to the authority of the Confederacy, they should not be called upon to serve against the Union, but be allowed to follow their peaceful pursuits without molestation during the continuance of the war. Relying upon these assurances, about forty of these hardy, but simple-minded mountaineers, emerged from their hiding-places, and delivered up their rifles. When thus rendered incapable of defense, they were forced into an old building, and then, under a strong guard, marched off to the jail at Asheville. There a number of them died from wretched fare and inhuman treatment, and, seeing no other way of escape, the remainder enlisted, but at the first opportunity deserted, and joined the Union ranks.

This was but the beginning of the perfidious acts committed by this Colonel Keith. Worse and bloodier deeds of his were soon to follow.

Alarm and indignation spread at once throughout the district, and Ellis could have organized within a fortnight a regiment of a thousand men; but what would that number have availed, surrounded by hostile forces, with no Union support nearer than Louisville, Kentucky. On their return trip from Swain county, Daniel Ellis had proposed that Reuben should co-operate with him in the conduct of his "underground road" for fugitives, by spreading a net-work of "stations" over the Alleghany region, and then extending the lines down the mountains into the very heart of the Confederacy. The project had met with the strong approval of Mrs. Hawkins, be- cause, she said, "One man thus added to the forces of the Union, will be equal to two subtracted from the strength of the Confederacy; and every soldier they send against you will be one withdrawn from their armies in the field. I see no way, Reuben, in which you can so effectively serve your neighbors, and your country."

Accordingly, Reuben Ellis had no sooner seen his wife and children safely returned to their home, than he dis- patched, under trusty pilots, a party of his neighbors to Dan Ellis; and this done, he visited, somewhat disguised, the entire mountain region; and even ventured so far within the Confederate lines as the lower country around Morganton. His custom was to travel by night, and to lay by during the day, in the woods, or at the house of some Union man in whom he had confidence. In sec- tions with which he was not familiar, his only guide was the stars, or a small pocket compass, and everywhere his only companion was a sixteen-repeating Henry carbine, the fellow to that of Daniel Ellis, which the famous guide on arriving at Warm Springs, had insisted upon presenting to him, to properly equip him for his hazardous employ- ment. Thus equipped, he soon revisited the vicinity of Waynesville, passed a day with Squire Plotts, and returned to him the horse which had served him so well in his escape from the gallows.

Directly after the visit of Dan Ellis very many of the youth of Madison county availed themselves of the facili- ties he offered to make their way to the Union lines; but the sons of Mrs. Hawkins remained at home, it being intended that, as soon as Reuben Ellis had established the "stations," they should act as "conductors" on the "underground road" through the mountain district, to Elizabethton, Tennessee; but, until that road was completed, they were forced to secrete themselves in the woods to avoid the conscript officers. All three did this, even the youngest, for such was the pressure for recruits, that the officials sometimes refused the evidence of the family Bible — if there chanced to be one — as to the age of a robust youth, able to carry a musket.

The food of the young men was taken to them by their mother, mounted upon the back of Sam, and accompanied by the hound which has been mentioned; but soon the intelligent dog so well learned the way that he was trusted to go with the rations unattended, if Mrs. Hawkins happened to be ill — and she was subject to frequent attacks of most distressing neuralgia. This fact became known to Colonel Keith, and the expedient he adopted to put a stop to the practice, and starve the lads into a surrender, had at least the merit of originality.

It was useless to attempt to follow the hound, for on several occasions the sagacious creature had baffled the most energetic pursuit. The only course was to stop the supplies at their source, and with this purpose, some twenty Confederates, under the sergeant who has been mentioned, appeared one morning at Mrs. Hawkins' door-way, proposing to quarter themselves upon her, that is — to subsist upon the widow's corn bread and bacon, for an indefinite time, or until her sons came in, and marched like men to the front to be targets for Union bullets.

"I can supply you with nothing," said Mrs. Hawkins. "My sons will starve rather than fight for the Confederacy. In their absence I shall have only women to gather in my crop, and it will, therefore, be small till another harvest — barely enough for my servant and myself. What is in the house, of course, you have the power to take; but you will not touch it, if you are gentlemen, and not thieves."

The orders of Colonel Keith clearly contemplated the eating up of the widow's substance, as the surest means of forcing her to submission, and her sons to a surrender. But, either the imperial bearing of Mrs. Hawkins, or some weak ambition to be deemed a gentleman, deterred the sergeant from a literal compliance with his instructions. He concluded to supply his own rations, but he set so close a watch upon the widow that it became impossible for her to furnish her sons with provisions. One of his men he detailed to dog her every footstep, the others he quartered day and night around the house, and in every one of its rooms, except the lady's bed-chamber. It thus was impossible for Mrs. Hawkins to hold with her sons any communication whatever.

This had been the situation of things for three or four days, when Sukey one morning appeared at the Hawkins mansion. The soldiers could not bridle the tongue of Mrs. Hawkins, and now, in the sergeant's presence, she told Sukey of the despicable espionage that was being practiced upon her. Sukey took the situation in at once, and on the spot resolved to thwart the design of the soldiers, by herself supplying food to the starving fugitives. By following Mrs. Hawkins into her bed-chamber, she learned their hiding-place, and instantly mounting her horse, she set out for her own dwelling. She was there emptying the contents of her larder into a huge meal-bag, when her husband entered the apartment — which was at once kitchen, dining-room, and sitting-room — and inquired of her what she was doing.

"Fixin' rations fur a better man nor ye ar'," answered Sukey, not pausing in her employment, "and let me warn ye, that if ye try ter find out whar I go, ter tell the sogers, I'll make Madison county too hot ter hold ye."

With not another word, she slung the bag upon her shoulder, then lifted it upon her horse, and mounting him herself, plunged directly into the forest. Her intimate acquaintance with the woods enabled her to locate the hiding-place of the young men, which was in a shallow cave that indented the side of a rocky ravine, about five miles back among the mountains. Thither she went by unfrequented ways, looking often back to be sure that she was not followed, and at the end of an hour, drew up in a clump of trees about a fourth of a mile from her destination. Then, tethering her horse to the limb of a tree, she made her way, with her bag upon her shoulder, through dense thickets of laurel and rhododendron, which the animal could not penetrate, till she came to the mouth of the cavern.

It was hidden by a thick growth of flowering shrubs, and was so low that it could be entered only on the hands and knees. Stooping down among the bushes, Sukey called in a subdued voice, "Aleck, Aleck, I ar' yere with some vittles." No answer coming, she called again and again, and then crept into the cavern.

When once in the cave she could stand upright, and by the dim light, which came in at the mouth, could see that the place was tenantless, but bore evidence of very recent occupation, in disordered beds, an open book on a block of wood, and a coffee-pot, empty of all but the dregs, which stood near a still-smouldering fire. Not a fragment of food could Sukey discover, and it was evident to her that the young men had drawn their entire sustenance for several days from the exhausted sediment of that one coffee-pot. She was anxious to personally assure them that she would, twice a week, bring them an abundance of provisions, but she dared not wait till their return, lest some chance passer-by in the forest should come upon her horse, and thus discover their hiding-place. Therefore, as soon as she had dragged the bag of provisions into the cavern, she rode back to the dwelling of Mrs. Hawkins.

The anxious mother was seated in her dining-room — an apartment on the opposite side of the hall from the sitting-room, of similar size, but less carefully furnished, and having for walls, the logs of the building, whitened and chinked with clay in the usual manner. Along its front and side were wide windows, but at its farther end was merely a door which communicated with the kitchen, and looked out upon a near-by corn-crib and corn-field. With Mrs. Hawkins were the sergeant and three of his men, the remainder of the squad being in the other rooms, and on the lawn in front of the dwelling.

14

The soldiers were conversing together, and giving them no heed Sukey passed directly to where Mrs. Hawkins was seated in the rear of the room, sewing, "I thort I'd come agin, ma'am," she said, as she took a chair by the open door in view of the corn-field. "Hit mout be I can't come ter morrer, so I thort I'd better do my stent ter day, by cuttin' ye some wood fur the kitchen fire."

"I am sorry to have you do such things for me, Sukey," replied Mrs. Hawkins, "I think you'd better leave the work to Martha and me."

"What! ma'am," exclaimed Sukey, "when ye has done so much fur me, and ye so weakly and sickly loike!"

She said no more, for happening to cast her eyes toward the corn-field she saw, coming through it, directly toward the house, and not a hundred yards away, the three sons of Mrs. Hawkins. Ignorant of the presence of the Confederates, and famishing for want of food, they had taken the desperate step of coming to their mother's dwelling. Hidden by the corn-crib, they could as yet be seen by no one in the room but Sukey; but in another moment they would turn the corner of that building, and be in plain view of the sergeant, and the three soldiers. Their fate hung upon a moment of time, and a woman's self-possession; but Sukey was equal to the emergency. Springing to her feet, and into the door-way, so as to more fully shield the young men from observation, she waved her arms toward them, shouting, "You ugly cat — go away — go away, I tell ye."

The young men dropped to the ground as if shot, and crept back into the corn-field, and turning to Mrs.

Hawkins, Sukey said, "That old cat was a drinkin' up yer milk, ma'am. Hain't I best put the pans onter the shelf in the kitchen?"

Knowing there was no cat around the premises, Mrs. Hawkins was conscious that it was her boys that Sukey was warning away, but no anxiety was expressed on her features, and she sat her chair as immovable as a marble statue. She merely said, "Yes, Sukey, I think the milk had better be put away. I'll thank you if you'll do it."

Sukey darted to the rear of the corn-crib, and there had a full view of the young men working their way noiselessly, in a crouching attitude, through the thick standing-corn, which then was six feet and more in height. By uttering a low mew, natural enough to have deceived one of the cat species, she attracted the attention of Aleck, who was in the rear of his brothers. She then made a gesture toward a huge chestnut, which, uprooted by a storm, was lying just in the edge of the ploughed field, and then another gesture toward the kitchen, making at the same time a movement of the hand to the mouth to indicate the act of eating. The pantomime was so cleverly done that Aleck smiled to the verge of laughter, and placing his hand upon his abdomen signified its emptiness, and that he understood her.

The fallen chestnut divided into two prongs a short distance from the butt; and into this crotch the young men crept, covering themselves with the dead leaves of the tree. They were so perfectly hidden that when Sukey, axe in hand — with a sack full of eatables under her arm — came to the trunk of the tree as if to gather chips, she had difficulty in discovering them. "Whar ar' ye boys?" she asked, in a loud whisper.

"In the crotch, Sukey," said Aleck. "You'd better come around to this side to avoid being seen."

She clambered over the huge trunk, and then, laying her sack at the feet of the boys, went busily to cutting up the branches of the tree, pausing every now and then in her work, to explain to them the situation. When the fugitives had eaten a hearty meal, and stowed away the remainder of the food, she filled her empty sack with chips, and returning with it to the house, said to Mrs. Hawkins, "Thar', ma'am, I've cut ye wood enough ter cook with till I come agin, the day arter ter morrer."

The young men laid by till nightfall, and then made their way to their lodgings in the cavern.

CHAPTER VII.

THROUGH THE LINES.

RETURNING to her dwelling, Sukey found her husband in close conference with a young gentleman wearing the gray uniform of the Confederacy. A sudden break occurred in their conversation when her presence was perceived, but she overheard the stranger say as she entered the door-way, "The General.will be sure to do as I tell you." Their subsequent remarks were upon unimportant subjects, about which the young Confederate could not be supposed to have ridden all the way from Asheville to consult a man of such limited general information as Parson Justin.

The presence of the stranger, the sudden pause in the conversation, and the constrained manner of the Parson, excited Sukey's suspicions, and the young man had no sooner gone than she asked her husband what it was that "the General" was to do. His answer, as she subsequently repeated it to Mrs. Hawkins, was that the Asheville commandant was his friend, and being so, had sent this young man to him to say, that, owing to the conscription having failed to produce the requisite number of recruits, it was soon to be extended to include all able-bodied men under the age of forty-five, except millers, physicians, and clergymen. Those classes would probably be exempt because food, physic, and the Christian religion, were deemed essential to the existence of the Confederacy. The General had thought it probable that the Parson would not be anxious to serve his country in the "imminent deadly breach," and, as he could not be exempted as a clergyman — he never having been ordained — the General suggested that he might possibly escape the draft by taking the superintendence of a grist-mill, near by upon the Ivy. The mill belonged to a Confederate officer, and the Parson could have the position, as the present manager was about to be transferred to some petty command in the service.

When Sukey inquired what price the Parson had to pay for so great a kindness, he answered, " Nothin'. The Ginral ar' my friend, an' he ar' doin' this eout uv cl'ar friendship."

This Sukey did not credit. She believed that the price he had agreed to pay was the betrayal of his neighbors. He was, she thought, to act as a spy to entrap them into the hands of the Confederates. This conviction she communicated to Mrs. Hawkins, but she carefully concealed it from her husband, for since she had learned to read, she had pondered much upon the precept, " Be ye wise as serpents," which she deemed peculiarly applicable to a condition of things wherein one's foes were those of his own household. Thus put upon her guard, Sukey observed extreme caution in conveying provisions to the sons of Mrs. Hawkins.

It was not many days before Reuben Ellis returned to the mountains, leading a company of fifty Union men whom he was piloting on to Dan Ellis at Elizabethton,

Tennessee. These men being joined by a still larger number from around the Ivy, he soon set out with them, and two of the Hawkins boys, to make the passage across the Alleghanies. Ellis was familiar with the route, and it was necessary that the Hawkins lads should become so, for the intention was that they should guide similar parties in future. Therefore, while Benjamin remained behind to receive any fugitives who might come in from the various stations which had been established by Reuben, Aleck and " Billy-Boy " went forward with the party.

All were on foot, each man carrying about ten days' rations ; but the younger Hawkins thought he could not trudge upwards of eighty miles, by ways seldom or never traveled, and over steep and rugged mountains, without his pony, Sam. Ellis objected to the horse as likely to betray them, but on being assured that the animal would keep silence, if he was so enjoined, and could be relied upon in the most precipitous and dangerous places, he reluctantly consented to his going with the party. To avoid exciting the suspicions of the guard at the mansion, Sukey was employed to borrow the pony of Mrs. Hawkins, and she did so on the plea of her need of a horse to use while the Parson was so much away with their own.

This little circumstance came near bringing disaster upon the expedition. Before conveying the pony to his youthful owner, Sukey lodged him overnight in the Parson's barn, after which he was neither seen nor heard of. The soldiers were doubtless informed of this by the Parson, when, on the following day, he made a formal call upon Mrs. Hawkins. To this conclusion that lady was led by the fact that before the Parson had left her house, one of the soldiers — taking a horse from her field without so much as saying "by your leave"— rode rapidly away in the direction of Colonel Keith's quarters.

On the following morning the sergeant surprised Mrs. Hawkins by courteously announcing that, inasmuch as his presence at her house had been productive of no result, he had orders from his colonel to remove his men from her premises.

Putting these several circumstances together, Mrs. Hawkins concluded that by some means — probably through the treachery of Justin — Colonel Keith had been led to suspect the intended hegira, and was calling in his men to prevent the escape of the fugitives. How strong a force he had was not known, for they were scattered in small squads throughout the district; but it was certain that it largely outnumbered the refugees, and might prove a serious obstruction to their progress. The soldiers had not been gone from her house an hour, when Mrs. Hawkins mounted a horse, and rode to the sequestered spot among the mountains where Ellis and the fugitives were lying concealed.

Ellis coincided in opinion with Mrs. Hawkins, but, to be assured of the real facts, he sent out several men in different directions to learn what movements had occurred among Keith's forces. The men returned with the uniform report that each separate squad of soldiers had been observed moving in the direction of Yancey county.

A short distance at the East a road leads directly through the mountains into Tennessee. This was the shortest and easiest route for the fugitives; but it was considerably traveled, and passing that way, by night or by day, so large a body of men could not escape observation. Therefore, Ellis decided to pursue a longer and rougher route along the eastern slope of the Alleghanies, and, avoiding the traveled roads, to guide his troop through the woods, and over the steep and rugged hills and mountains with which the way was obstructed. The movement of the soldiers toward Yancey county indicated that Keith had ⁻divined his intentions, and was preparing to waylay him; but Ellis had no alternative, so, he set out on a starless night in early August, knowing that only by extreme caution, and sleepless vigilance, could he break through the meshes of the net in which he was enveloped.

Without encountering any special obstacle, the company had gone some twelve miles, and entered the borders of Yancey county, when they arrived at the base of two steep and rugged mountains, the Big Bald, and the Sugar Loaf, which rose directly in their path, and were nearly a mile in height. To avoid a long detour, Ellis had intended to climb a sloping gap which lies between these mountains, but the place was one that Keith would naturally select for an ambuscade, and he was unwilling to enter it until it had been reconnoitred. For this service " Billy-Boy " volunteered; the company halting in the forest while he went forward with his pony on a noiseless walk.

The lad had proceeded but a short distance up the gap when, intermingled with the tree trunks, and not two

15

hundred yards away, he saw what appeared to be several hundred stumps, standing closely together, and all about of the size of a man's body. Shielded by the dense foliage, the boy halted his horse, and scanned the stumps as narrowly as was possible in the darkness. He soon perceived they were endowed with motion, and that some of them were in attitudes not natural to chopped-off timber. Noiselessly wheeling his horse, and keeping altogether in the shadow of the trees, he walked slowly back to the waiting company.

Without a moment's delay, Ellis led his men about a mile back upon the route they had come, and then took a northerly course toward the Big Butt Mountain. It was distant about eight miles, but the troop reached its lower slopes just as the day was breaking, and climbing then its rugged face for a mile or more, they went into camp in a dense grove of laurels. Here they prepared their breakfast, and, being much fatigued, were soon soundly asleep among the matted bushes.

While they slept Ellis and Alexander Hawkins pushed on up the mountain to discover some clear spot from which they could view the surrounding country. Such a spot they found on a steep ledge of rocks from whose flinty surface the rain had worn just enough soil to support a scanty growth of stunted spruce and hemlock. Here, looking over the tops of the tall trees below them, they saw, about eight miles away, the gleaming gun-barrels of two distinct bodies of soldiery. One body appeared to be emerging from the gap the younger Hawkins had so fortunately explored, the other was about a

mile to the westward, and both were moving on lines
that would converge in the highway which passed along
the southern base of the Big Butt, about two miles from
where they were standing. This highway the refugees
had been obliged to cross to make the ascent of the
mountain, and, as the passage of a hundred and twenty
men through matted undergrowth, leaves of necessity a
very distinct trail, it was morally certain that the route
they had taken would be discovered. The two bodies of
soldiers numbered not less than five hundred, and between them the refugees had passed on the preceding
night, at a probable distance from the more westerly
one, of only a few hundred yards.

The only safe thing for Ellis to do, was to count upon
discovery, and place his men in a position where they
might repel the onslaught of four times their own number. Such a position was the ledge on which he was
standing. It was a narrow shelf, with at its back an
abrupt cliff several hundred feet high, and the ascent to
it was so steep as to be approachable by a man only on
his hands and knees. The objection to the position —
inasmuch as Ellis desired to avoid a conflict — was that a
body of men stationed upon it would be in plain view,
through several openings in the trees upon the lower
ground, of any one coming near to it, from a southerly
direction. But, the soldiers were rapidly approaching, and there was no time to select a better position;
therefore, leaving Hawkins to observe their movements,
Ellis hurried down the ledge to arouse the sleeping
refugees.

The entire company was soon upon their feet, and following Ellis down the mountain upon the same trail by which they had ascended to their encampment. When within a hundred yards of the highway Ellis gave the word to halt, and ordered every man to take off his shoes, and, in scattering order, and leaving no trail, to follow him again up the mountain. This he did to baffle pursuit, and give the impression that his company had there taken to the highway.

It was two miles of steep climbing, and, on several occasions, the pony, Sam, had to be almost lifted up some sharp acclivity; but at the end of nearly an hour the whole company arrived safely at the foot of the selected position. Here, a difficulty not before thought of presented itself. By no possible means could Sam be got up the precipice. He had been trained to kneel at the behest of his master, but such a thing as climbing a precipice upon his hands and knees, was not yet included among the pony's accomplishments. Therefore sadly the boy led him a short distance away into the woods — sadly, because if there was to be a "scrimmage," he longed to be in it.

While the men were making their toilsome way up to the rocky shelf, Alexander Hawkins had seen the two bodies of soldiers come together, and then, after a brief halt, move forward to the highway. Now and then they were hidden by some projecting mountain spur, but their course was steadily forward, and if they did not turn back, they would soon be abreast of the point from which the refugees had ascended the mountain. When the last refugee had climbed the ledge, the soldiers were not more than four miles distant; but so overcome were the fugitives with the fatigue of their tramp of twenty miles through ploughed fields and dense undergrowth, stumbling in the darkness every now and then over rocks and fallen trees, that as one after another gained the rocky shelf, he sank to the ground, and regardless of his danger, fell at once into a deep slumber. Soon Ellis and Alexander Hawkins were the only individuals standing erect in the entire company.

With deep concern Ellis observed the exhaustion of his men, and with keen anxiety watched the soldiers approach the point where the refugees had crossed the highway. There they halted, and about three-fourths of the number dismounted, and took the trail which led up to the encampment in the grove of laurels. The two watchers sank to their knees behind a couple of dwarf hemlocks; but they kept their eyes riveted upon the moving soldiery. Soon they saw them arrive at the spot, carefully inspect the bushes, and, then, after a brief pause, as if for rest, retrace their steps down the mountain. All now hung upon whether the soldiers should observe the trail of the fugitives where they had turned to make the ascent to the ledge of rocks. In breathless suspense the two men watched their movements. When they saw them pass the point without discovering it, they could have shouted for joy — but shouting might be heard, and, moreover, was not in order, for Keith had not yet given over the pursuit, nor were the fugitives yet out of danger.

Remounting their horses, the soldiers now pressed on up the high-road to lay, as Ellis supposed, other ambuscades for the approaching night, into which they hoped to entrap the tired refugees. Another dangerous tramp was therefore before his men, and for it they would need all their strength; so Ellis let them sleep on while he and Hawkins discussed the best course to pursue in the circumstances.

The Big Butt Mountain is not one of the highest of the Alleghanies, but it extends ten miles from east to west, and only by a weary climb of five miles can one reach its summit. The refugees were encamped on its southern slope, at the foot of which the road pursued by the soldiers winds through a wooded region till it reaches the Toe river, where it opens upon a broad valley tenanted by a considerable farming population. On that route, therefore, the fugitives would have before them, not only the soldiers, but perhaps an unfriendly people, some of whom might observe and report their movements.

The northern slope of the mountain, on the contrary, is covered by an unbroken forest, traversed by no road, and occupied by only one dwelling — the cabin of a white man whom Ellis had visited a few years before, when on a hunting expedition. As it was now more important to throw off pursuit, than to make progress, would it not be well to scale the mountain, and encamp in some secluded spot on its northern slope, till the refugees were sure that Colonel Keith had turned back to Madison county? This course being decided upon, Ellis and Hawkins stretched themselves upon the flinty rock for a few hours' slumber.

They awoke about two hours after noon, and, rousing the men, set out to climb in a zig-zag course the rugged face of the mountain. Their way was everywhere obstructed by rocks, fallen trees, and sharp acclivities, and the feet of many of the men being badly swollen from the travel of the previous night, they made but slow progress. Not till half an hour before sunset did they reach the level, treeless space that forms the summit of the Big Butt, and look off upon the wilderness of forest-clad mountains which fill the entire field of vision. It is a magnificent panorama; but it had no attractions for these hunted men, who saw, gleaming in the sun a few miles away, along the winding Toe, the stacked arms of their numerous pursuers.

There was no water on the summit, and water was indispensable, not only to quench the thirst of the fainting men, but to bathe their feet and limbs, sadly torn and bruised as they were by the prostrate trees and sharp rocks, over which they had so often stumbled in the darkness. But Ellis knew of a spring, copious and never failing, which gushes out of the mountain side about five hundred yards from the summit, and is one of the sources of Devil's creek — the euphonious name of a picturesque stream which flows into Toe river about twelve miles away. Around the pool formed by this spring the men were soon gathered, laving their feet in the ice-cold water.

They formed a picturesque group. More than three thousand feet above the sea, the elevation was too great for the larger growth of deciduous trees, but above their heads rose a majestic grove of balsam, soaring, in some instances, a hundred and fifty feet into the air; and around them, on all sides, were dense thickets of laurel and rhododendron, loaded with their fragrant pink and pale-yellow blossoms. For a circuit of about a hundred feet around the spring the ground had been trodden bare of shrubbery, by the countless wild animals which had frequented it for innumerable centuries. And this bare space was covered by a thick green sward, excellent fod-der for Sam, and a soft bed for the tired men who were now gathered upon it, some seated on the ground, some leaning upon their rifles, and some standing erect, and peering through the trees at the camp of their pursuers, in absolute descent, and nearly half a mile below them. The men were all in the prime of life, or early manhood — tall, erect, and muscular, with rugged faces, and a resolute look which told that they would brave all things rather than submit to what they deemed oppression.

A few of them stood in a group looking down at the distant soldiers, and earnestly consulting together; but after a time they turned back to where Ellis was seated upon the grass, quietly eating his supper, and one said to him: "Captain, we uns doan't 'xzactly loike this bein' hunted down loike wild critters."

"Nor do I," said Ellis. "It isn't altogether pleasant; but I don't see how we can help it."

"We uns reckon we know a way ter holp hit," said the man, "Jest light down on them fellers before mornin'."

"Well, that might finish some of them, and scatter the rest," answered Ellis; "but I doubt if it would help you to get through to the Union lines. I think we had better not have a fight unless it is forced upon us."

"But we uns karn't stand this skulkin' much longer — hit'r. agin natur'."

"Well," said Ellis, "I'll tell you what I propose to do, and then you can tell me what you think of it. Those men have failed to find our tracks in the road, and are convinced that we are still upon this mountain. I conclude so from their placing their camp where they can head us off, whether we leave the mountain on this side, or the other. They will scour this whole region for us to-morrow, and then, if we are discovered, we can fight them with the chances greatly in our favor; for I know a spot on the creek below here, where we can completely hide, and which, if they find it, we can hold against twice their number."

The men were satisfied with this explanation, and soon the whole number were gathered in little groups upon the grass, engaged in cheerful conversation, and giving, apparently, no thought to what might happen on the morrow.

On the following morning the refugees ate their breakfasts without building a fire, lest its smoke should betray their position; and soon afterward, the men on the lookout reported a movement at Keith's encampment. The soldiers appeared to be saddling their horses, and soon they were seen to move away along the road down Toe river. "They are coming this way, as I expected," said Ellis. "It will take them all of three hours to get this far up the mountain; but we had better be getting into hiding."

16

A majority of the men had not yet resumed their shoes, and directing the others to remove theirs, and every one to step in the running water of the streamlet, Ellis now led the company down the creek, leaving, however, a small squad behind to remove every vestige of the encampment. Every small article was carefully gathered up, the trodden grass was coaxed to stand erect with small twigs, and then "Billy-Boy" led Sam several times over the cleared space, to give the sward the appearance of having been crushed by the feet of the bears, wolves, and panthers, which were known to infest the mountain in large numbers.

About a thousand feet farther down the creek, and at the mouth of a narrow ravine, with walled, precipitous sides, was a large grove of laurels, taller, and denser than any the men had seen, and growing closely down to the margin of the stream. In this grove the men were told to secrete themselves, carefully replacing every twig they were obliged to remove in effecting an entrance. It was slow work, but by the end of an hour all were snugly housed among the laurels — even "Billy-Boy" and Sam, who were stretched together at full length upon the ground, the boy's head resting upon the horse's neck, and both fast approaching that condition of slumber which is said to "keep one eye open."

Ellis and the older Hawkins had remained behind, to observe the movements of the soldiers. Standing at the summit, they soon saw the troop divide, about three-fourths of them striking directly westward into the forest, while the other fourth remained on the bank of the Toe, about five hundred yards above the mouth of Devil's creek.

"Do you see what that means, Aleck?" asked Ellis. "They are keeping those men there to be ready to head us off if we attempt to leave the mountain, and they have scattered those single horsemen along the road in their rear, to give notice of our movements. The squad that is coming this way will break into small parties, and only one party will come up this creek. What a splendid chance it will be to make hash of the whole of them — we could easily thrash the squad that comes this way, the firing would attract the others here, but they would come up separately, and we could cut them off in detail. What do you say, Aleck? The men now are thoroughly rested, and would fight desperately."

"I think it had better be done," said Hawkins. "It would clear our way into Tennessee."

"That is exactly what I fear it would not do," answered Ellis. "The mountain people all through here are for the Union; but I am told the whole region swarms with soldiers, trying to force the lying-out men into the Rebel ranks. I am afraid a fight would bring so many of them upon us that we couldn't possibly get through. I think we had better avoid a collision if we can; if we cannot, you and I will not be responsible for the consequences."

Ellis took a position in the laurels near to Billy and the pony, both of whom appeared to be soundly asleep. "Wake up, Billy," said Ellis, "you'll need to have all your wits about you to keep this pony quiet."

"That's all you know about natural history," replied Billy, opening his eyes, and sitting upright. "Sam will be deader'n a door-nail. Let me show you." Then addressing the horse the boy exclaimed, "Wake up, Sam." The pony opened his eyes, raised his head from the ground, and looked at his master. "Now, Sam," said Billy, "play dead." Instantly the pony laid his head again upon the ground, closed his eyes, stretched out his limbs, and became absolutely motionless, not even his breathing being perceptible. "Now, Reuben," continued Billy, "you might kick him, or even roll him over, and not get a sign of life out of him. But no one else can handle him as I can."

"Well, he is a knowing animal," said Ellis.

"Knowing!" answered Billy, "he knows every thing except the ten commandments, and those he keeps better than most human beings."

Speaking only in low whispers the fugitives waited for perhaps two hours, when sounds were heard coming up the creek, as of a body of men stumbling, now and then, over the loose stones that paved the channel. Rapidly the sounds came nearer, and soon about a hundred soldiers, led by a tall man in the uniform of a Confederate major, passed silent, and in single file, before the mouth of the ravine.

The Confederates had been gone half an hour when they returned in a reverse order — the major being in the rear, with another officer. As the two came abreast, and within a hundred yards of the hidden refugees, the major said to the other, "They have been thar, though they've covered up their tracks with amazin' smartness. They must be now on some part of the mountain. D—n the orders; I wish the colonel would listen to me, and—" The remainder of the sentence was lost in the distance. While he said this not less than fifty rifles were pointed directly at him, and a slight pressure of the finger upon any one of them would have sent him into eternity.

As the soldiers passed out of hearing, Ellis said to those about him, "I know that man; his name is Irving. He lives on the 'Chucky river, and is one of the biggest scoundrels in existence." Subsequent events showed that Irving was a fit comrade to the bloody-minded Keith.

In about half an hour the men were allowed to emerge from their hiding place, and return to the encampment on the summit of the mountain; but a couple of sentinels were left behind at the laurel bushes, to give warning in case the soldiers should be heard again ascending the creek. Nothing further of importance occurred till about two hours before sunset, when the troops were observed to emerge from the woods which hid the base of the mountain, and to join the men who had been left upon Toe river. Then the whole body forded the river, and rode rapidly down the road which, passing a mile or two to the east of the hamlet of Erwin, leads directly to Jonesborough, Tennessee. This movement Ellis did not understand, but he deemed the opportunity favorable for an escape from the mountain; and accordingly, in a few moments the refugees, with him and Aleck at their head, were making their slow way down the streamlet.

It wanted still an hour of sunset when Ellis halted the troop in a group of trees about half a mile from the foot of the mountain, and said to them, "A man that I know lives a little way below. He may have talked with some of the soldiers. Hawkins and I will go down, and see if we can learn from him the meaning of their movements. Stay here, unless you hear our rifles."

The house stood in a cultivated clearing of about ten acres, and was of logs, with a slab roof, held down by long weight-poles. It was approached by only a narrow path, and had never so much as seen a wheeled vehicle, it being all of three miles from any highway. Ellis and Hawkins had no sooner entered the path, than a dozen ferocious dogs sprang from before the dwelling, and set up a dismal howling. Soon a woman, clad in decent homespun, came to the door, and calling off the dogs, said to the visitors, "How d'ye, strangers!"

"How are *you*, Mrs. Pollard," said Ellis, advancing toward her.

"Lord ha' massy! Rube Ellis, ar' thet ye?" exclaimed the woman, in great surprise. "Why, we uns hearn tell ye war strung up by the measly Rebels."

"No," answered Reuben, "I managed to give them the slip. But where is your husband?"

"In the bush, jest ahind uv the barn. Ye sees, he hev ter tuck ter the bush when ary one is seed a comin', 'case the conscript galoots ar' thicker round hyar nur bugs in a feather-bed. Come inter the house, and tuck cheers, while I blow fur him. He'll be powerful glad ter greet ye."

While the woman took down a cow's-horn that hung at the door-way, Reuben and Aleck entered the dwelling. It had two rooms on the ground floor, and a loft overhead, approached by a ladder in the corner. A fire of pine knots, by which the woman was preparing supper, was blazing on the broad stone hearth, and near it were several small children, with hands and faces not quite so grimy as is common to the juvenile mountaineers of that latitude. Three rough bedsteads, piled high with feather-beds and well-worn quilts, were set against the walls, which were white-washed and chinked with clay, and here and there ornamented with engravings extracted from some illustrated newspaper, yellow with age or dampness. From a window was suspended, in lieu of a curtain, a glaring, highly-colored pill advertisement. In the center of the well-scoured puncheon-floor stood a pine table, on which were a pot of coffee, a plate of fried bacon, and another of sweet potatoes and corn-pone, all smoking hot and waiting to be eaten.

Evidently, the house was occupied by a family that is typical of a large population in this mountain region. Ignorant, unambitious, and hidden away in forest recesses, these people are content to let the world jog on its noisy way, so long as they can glean a scanty livelihood from their little clearings, and the game they can bring down with their shot-guns. Being outside the sphere of schools and churches, they have no learning, nor any religion beyond what is natural to man in the most primitive condition. They pay no taxes, recognize no political authority, and live in a pure state of natural liberty, regulated only by the savage law of *lex talionis* — an eye for an eye, a tooth for a tooth, and a plug of tobacco for another plug — at the borrower's convenience.

The man who now entered the cabin was tall, broad shouldered, and of splendid physical proportions. His hair and beard were long and black, and he wore a brown hunting-shirt, homespun trousers, high-top boots, and a slouch hat — which he did not take the trouble to remove from his head when he grasped Reuben by the hand, almost shouting, "Why, I'm powerful glad ter see ye. I thort ye war a dingnation fule; but hit's clar ye hev sense enuff ter keep yer head on yer shoulders."

"Why did you think me a fool?" asked Ellis, laughing.

"'Case ye tuck sides in this hyar scrimmage. Let 'em fite hit eout 'mong tharselves. The world'll get along if all uv 'em gwo ter th' dogs."

In this, he expressed the political sentiment of, perhaps, a majority of his district. However, Ellis was not there to discuss such subjects, but to ascertain, if he could, the object of Keith's march in the direction of Tennessee. The native could not tell him; he had not conversed with, nor even been seen by, any of the soldiers, but his wife had, and she now said, " I kin tell ye, Mr. Ellis. They're bound fur Greenville. Two uv 'em stopped hyar, an' 'sisted on me gittin' 'em dinner. One was thet devil, Sam Irving, from over ter Washington county; an' he done nuthin' but swar through the hull meal, 'case th' regimen' was ordered ter onct over ter Tennessee. He wanted ter stay long enuff ter kotch an' hang, a lot of Madison county men, as he say ar' a hidin' in this mounting."

His route now being cleared of Keith and his mounted militia, Ellis pressed forward rapidly — lying-by in the woods during the day — and on the morning of the sixth day the refugees met Dan Ellis at the rendezvous he had appointed — the old forge in the vicinity of Elizabethton, Tennessee. There Reuben Ellis, and the Hawkins boys, left the refugees, and returned without accident to Madison county, while Dan Ellis led the weary men forward to Kentucky.

It was a ten days' experience of narrow escapes and almost incredible hardships, during which they were forty-eight hours without food; but at last, faint and famishing, their clothing torn to shreds, their faces and limbs scratched and bleeding, and their feet so swollen that they could scarcely walk, the entire company entered the Union lines in safety. For eighteen days not one of them had been within a human habitation, and the first dwelling which Dan Ellis, and a small party, visited was not of a kind to impress them with very high ideas of Kentucky civilization. It was in the mountains of east Kentucky, and, as the family is a fair representative of a large class in that region, I subjoin a description which Daniel Ellis has written of the reception he met there.

"The place," he writes, "had quite a forbidding appearance; but the men were very tired and hungry, and said they were compelled to rest. Every thing about the premises had the indelible mark of filthiness, and cer-

17

tainly none but hungry dogs, or half-starved men, could
have had the stomach to eat at that dirty-looking place.
But under the stress of circumstances, we resolved to
try one meal, at any rate.   When I entered the house the
first object that attracted my observation was an old
woman, sitting in a corner of the fire-place, smoking a
pipe.   She was ragged and barefooted, her feet were as
scaly and black with dirt as a toad's back, and her ankles
(for her dress was too short to conceal them) looked like
a couple of rusty gun barrels.   Her hair had surely never
been combed, for it stood out in a thousand directions —
in short she was begrimed with dirt from head to foot."

"There were also two girls, who seemed to be about
eighteen years of age, who ran into another room, but
soon came back, each one habited in a calico dress, which
was so thin, and their under-dress so scarce — if indeed
there was any under-dress at all — that their forms were
distinctly visible through their scanty clothing."

"They commenced making preparations for supper,
and one of the girls, accompanied by an old, and very
poor, hound, started in pursuit of a chicken, which, after
a long time, they succeeded in catching, when the girl
pulled its head off, and laid it on a table.   Soon a large
cat jumped up and dragged it off to the floor, when two
other cats seized it by each wing, and the three ran out of
the house with it, and attempted to get under the floor.
But all at once a hound-puppy stopped them in their
course, caught the chicken by the tail, and there they
stood, each one striving for the mastery, with awful growls
and snarls.   To end the dispute one of the girls made a

sudden dash with the fire-shovel upon the squad of car-nivorous animals, and recaptured the prize, which she at once proceeded to prepare for our supper!"

"We purchased a small hog, and had it cooked, and we also had a plenty of corn bread; but it was baked out of meal which was badly spoiled, and consequently was not very palatable. To cap the climax of dainties, they cooked a quantity of green cabbage, full of worms, and with not a particle of salt to the whole unsavory mess."

"No person knows what he can be induced to eat, until he has suffered for several days and nights from the most excessive hunger."

"After supper we began to pile about the floor to sleep, for the beds were so ragged and dirty, that they looked unpromising, and I had no doubt were well supplied with vermin. We slept until morning, but did not stay to breakfast. We paid our bill, which was fifty cents each, and then set out for Manchester, Kentucky."

In a very few days after their arrival at Manchester, every one of the refugees had enlisted in the Union army.

CHAPTER VIII.

A TRAGEDY.

In the absence of Colonel Keith's regiment, the operations of the "underground road" assumed a remarkable degree of activity. Reuben Ellis had formed connections as far east as Burke county, and west to the State line in Graham and Swain counties, and from all the intervening districts there soon poured in to the rendezvous in Madison county, the best war material of the mountain region. It is impossible to state the emigration with any degree of accuracy, but during the six months next succeeding the first trip of Ellis into Tennessee, it could not have been less than one thousand.

The extent of Ellis's operations was probably not suspected by the Confederate authorities. He was known to be somewhere in the district, and a reward was offered for his capture, and also for that of the Hawkins boys, but it failed to tempt any one of the many hundreds who knew of their resorts, to either molest or betray them. Various small squads were sent into Madison county to secure their arrest, and some of these squads came directly under the guns of larger bodies of the refugees, but, acting on the advice of Mrs. Hawkins, Ellis invariably allowed them to pass by unmolested.

As soon as it was known that no permanent force of Confederates was any longer in the neighborhood, many of the out-liers emerged from their hiding-places to aid their wives and daughters to gather in their harvests, but they ventured out with great caution, and adopted a code of signals by which the neighbors gave them warning of the approach of the soldiery. But it was soon observed that the appearance of any considerable number was sure to be speedily followed by the visit of an armed force from Asheville. The connection of these events was especially noticed directly after about ten of the refugees had, during two entire days, worked at gathering in the crops of Mrs. Hawkins. It was evident that there was a spy in the neighborhood, but who he was could not be conjectured.

It was not supposed to be Parson Justin. He, good man, was high above suspicion. In the beginning of the disturbances, when all were called upon to define their position, the question had been asked why he did not declare his principles, and the answer given was, " Princerpuls! How kin he 'clar 'em when he hain't nary a princerpul." This appears to have been the universal opinion, and it was thought that he was " sitting the fence " in readiness to spring to whichever side should come out uppermost.

But public sentiment in regard to the Parson speedily changed after he took charge of the mill upon the Ivy. It soon came to be remarked that if he had no political faith, he had some practical Christianity, for he suddenly blossomed out a good Samaritan. No lone woman who, in the absence of her husband, had been obliged to sow and reap her own little harvest, ever came to him

with a single bushel of corn, but it was returned to her
in two bushels of meal, which, if it proved too heavy for
the woman to carry, the Parson would load upon his
horse, and taking her up behind him, would "tote" it off
to her humble dwelling, discoursing on the way somewhat as follows: "Yes, Mary, my dear child, hev no
fears, fur so long ez John ar' away, ye shill not want — yer
single bag uv corn shill be loike th' widder's cruse uv oil
ez never failed ; fur I loves all th' brave boys ez ar' away
a fightin' fur thar kentry. These ar' troublous times,
Mary, an' 'taint egzactly prudent fur a preacher uv th'
gospil loike me ter be too free uv his princerpuls ; but ye
kin tell John them ar' my sentimints — an' whar ar' John
now, Mary ? up thar to Barnet's Cove ?"

"No, Parson," Mary replies, " 'Twar only last night
thet Rube Ellis sent Billy Hawkins ter tole me ez John
hed got through, all safe an' sound, ter th' Union lines.
I was awful sorry ter hev John gwo, but he 'lowed hit
war his duty — he say ez how when all th' rich men war a
gwine agin thar kentry, hit war th' bounden duty uv
uvery pore man ter stand up fur hit.   I kinder thort ez
he done, but — hit ar' awful lonesome fur me an' my
little chil'ren witheout John."

"I kin b'lieve ye, Mary," rejoins the Parson, "but
'taint fur frum yer house ter th' camp on Rich Mounting ;
ye kin gwo thar most ary time, an' git news of John
frum Reuben or th' Hawkins boys."

"I doan't know," she answers, "ez thar is ary camp
ter Rich Mounting, an' ef I done know hit, I'd nuver
gwo thar, fur a price are sot onter Reuben an' th' boys'

heads, an' ef some un without ary soul shud betray 'em, they mout lay hit ter me, an' thet wud break my heart — they hev been so good ter me. Why, John an' me never cud hev got in th' crap ef they hadn't sent men ter holp us; fur all th' wuck hed ter be done in one night by moonlight."

With questions like these the Parson plied the humble recipients of his bounty, and if they had not been so very simple-minded, they might have detected the motive of his rare, though not costly, generosity — not costly to him, for he merely took from the rich to give to the poor, filched from the meal-bags of the well-conditioned to fill the aprons of their less fortunate neighbors. While acting thus he could safely announce Union sentiments, for he was merely furthering the designs of the Asheville officials, who had supplied him with an assistant expressly to afford him leisure to go about delivering meal to poor women, whom his sham generosity might entrap into a betrayal of their husbands.

This assistant was a stalwart, broad-shouldered fellow, well enough endowed physically, but apparently deficient in intellectual equipment. He had a way of mumbling his words, and at times his utterances were so incoherent that it was impossible to understand him. But Sukey thought she detected in him indubitable evidence of shamming, and this, coupled with his absence on hunting excursions directly prior to every appearance of the soldiery, led her to say to Mrs. Hawkins, " He haint no natural, ma'am· He ar' a spy, sent hyar ter holp the Parson ter git holt uv his naboors. Doan't ye think, ma'am, th' camp had better be moved ter onct from Rich Mounting? Th' Parson 'spects hit ar' thar, an' he ar' mean nuff ter sell his best friend fur the reward ez is sot on Reuben an' th' boys.'' The camp was removed, and more than ordinary care was taken to prevent its new location becoming known in the neighborhood.

On the 1st of November, 1862, the conscription limit was extended so as to embrace all able-bodied men under the age of forty-five. This at once multiplied the number of " half-faced cabins " that were scattered about upon the mountains, and sent additional fugitives upon the long and perilous march to the Union lines; yet, it did not materially change the aspect of this mountain community, nor add to the recruits it furnished to the forces of the Confederacy. Now and then a conscript was captured, and forced into the ranks, but only to desert at the first opportunity.

So many men had evaded both the first and second conscriptions that by the winter of 1862–63, it was found necessary to adopt more stringent measures to augment the armies of the Confederacy, and Colonel Keith was again detailed to bring into the ranks the lying-out conscripts in the mountains of Tennessee and North Carolina. He re-entered Madison county on January 19, 1863, and then began a series of massacres which, so far as I know, have had no parallel in civilized warfare on the American Continent. He openly proclaimed that his men had orders to shoot on sight all conscripts who did not at once voluntarily report themselves at his head-quarters, and enter the ranks, thereby outlawing every able-bodied man in the district.

If I were writing a history of Madison county, I should now have to relate, in harrowing detail, how helpless women were mercilessly beaten, and otherwise maltreated, for refusing to betray their husbands and fathers, and how aged men, and half-grown boys, were hanged to trees, and shot down in cold blood, by the monsters Keith and Irving, with attending cruelties that would have put to shame an Apache savage. The atrocities shocked the Confederate authorities, but when they called Major Irving to account for his slaughter of innocent children his only reply was : " It was right to kill all the boys to prevent them from growing up to be Federal soldiers and bushwhackers, for the Southern soldiers to have to fight."

The mention of these things seems necessary to show what these people endured rather than deny their country, or betray its friends. But I need say no more, except that during four brief periods, covering, all told, less than two months of time, the butcher Keith slaughtered forty-seven unarmed men and harmless children, within the limits of one narrow district of the Carolina mountains. His acts fully justified the remark of Mrs. Hawkins to Reuben Ellis, " You can serve your country and humanity in no way so well as by helping every man and boy to get away from Madison county."

When Colonel Keith re entered the district Reuben Ellis was absent piloting a party of refugees into Tennessee, and Alexander Hawkins was on the eve of setting out, from the new camp near the Shelton Laurel, with another party of a hundred and ten men from Madison, and the adjoining counties. But young Hawkins was

18

cautious, as well as bold, and distrusting his ability to elude, with so large a body, so watchful an enemy as Colonel Keith, he delayed his departure until the return of Ellis, who was daily and hourly expected. While he was thus waiting, Sukey rode up to the camp late one day with tidings that his mother was suddenly seized with a dangerous illness. As has been said, Mrs. Hawkins was subject to painful attacks of neuralgia, but this attack was more serious than any she had ever experienced, and it wrenched her system so severely that Sukey feared she could not survive it.

Without delay the three young men set out for their home. They went on foot, and along by-paths, for Keith's men were now in all the settlements. They found their mother lying on an improvised bed in the dining-room, and suffering the extremest tortures. The oldest son had over her a singular magnetic influence. By holding her hands in his, and putting his will intently and strongly upon her, he had often brought her relief while in the severest spasms. He now sat down by her side, and exerted all his powers, while his brothers stood anxiously by, watching every movement of the sufferer. The struggle was long, and for hours it seemed as if tranquillity would never again revisit her torn and disordered nerves; but at last her head sank back upon her pillow, and she lay free from pain but utterly exhausted.

That mysterious thing which we call life was now flickering low in its socket, and the danger was that she would die from sheer exhaustion. So, the young man still sat by his mother's side, holding her hands, and thus giving to her of that subtle fluid which, it may be, is the connecting link between the soul and its earthly tenement. Slowly it crept along her overstrained nerves, gradually giving them the strength and tone by which they transmit to the spirit correct impressions of sensible objects; and at last, just as the gray dawn began to steal through the crevices of the carefully-closed window-shutters, she sat erect in bed, and spoke with something of her accustomed coherence and animation.

Mrs. Hawkins was now out of danger, and her sons were convinced that she would experience the rapid recovery which usually attends acute nervous attacks; but, the sun having risen, they deemed it unsafe to leave the house until nightfall. Accordingly, the shutters of the dining-room were allowed to remain closed, and directions were given to the faithful woman who had served Mrs. Hawkins ever since the death of her husband, to admit no one to the house except Sukey. To all others she was to say that her mistress could not possibly receive visitors.

Soon Sukey came, but seeing that Mrs. Hawkins was in no need of her services, she said she would take a little food from the kitchen, and go to the barn, where, in the loft, she would watch until night, to give warning in case any of the soldiers should come near the dwelling. Not long afterward the old-fashioned knocker at the hall-door sounded, and Parson Justin announced that he had come all the way on foot from the mill, to inquire after the condition of Mrs. Hawkins. The servant answered him as she had been instructed, and he left the house,

going, however, direct to the barn, where he very deliberately put a saddle and bridle upon the horse which
Sukey had ridden from the mill, and stabled by the side
of that of Mrs. Hawkins.   This Sukey saw him do, and
then ride away, not by the road to their home, but in the
direction of Yancey county, where, some eight miles
away, Colonel Keith had his head-quarters.

This circumstance set Sukey to thinking. Had the
Parson enough concern for Mrs. Hawkins — or for any
human being — to induce him to trudge five miles through
six inches of snow merely to ascertain her condition?
And, why had he gone off in the direction of the Confederate head-quarters, when every step of his way took him
farther from the mill? Had he inferred that the dangerous illness of the mother would bring the sons to their
home, and, from the closed shutters, that they were then
actually in the dwelling? And, convinced of this, was
he then on his way to betray them to Colonel Keith?
The thought gave Sukey intense concern, and instantly
she came down from the hay-mow, and repaired to the
dwelling to tell her fears to the young men and their
mother.

Though she considered Sukey's estimate of Justin
not far from the truth, Mrs. Hawkins could not believe him so lost to human feeling as to betray the sons
of a woman to whom he owed so large a debt of grati-
tude; and Alexander remarked that the coming of the
soldiers was at the worst only a probable danger, while
leaving the house by daylight was a positive one, for it
would be impossible to escape observation in crossing the

quarter of a mile of clearing which lay between the house and the nearest forest. This last consideration decided the young men to remain with their mother until nightfall.

In the genial society of her sons Mrs. Hawkins found her strength rapidly returning, and swiftly the hours flew by, for they had very much to say to one another. Never before, since the war first visited the region, had mother and sons passed an entire day together. At length night came, and with it Sukey to remind the young men that it had arrived, and to urge their immediate departure. This done, she set out alone to trudge on foot to her home through the untrodden snow of a dense forest, with neither moon nor star to light her way.

But still the young men lingered. "Something seemed to hold them," said Mrs. Hawkins to me in recounting the circumstance, "and a sort of spell was on me, too. I did not know, but I felt, that it was to be our last hour on earth together; and my mother's heart clung to them, and would not let them go."

While they thus stood, saying their last words to one another, there came a swaying in the shrubbery before the house — something like the low rustle of the wind among the trees — and bending her ear to the sound, the mother said, "Do you hear that, boys? We are surrounded."

The part of the house occupied by the dining-room had been the first portion erected, and it was provided with a door which opened directly from the room upon the front lawn. This door was now never used, but it was not so strongly secured as the one which opened from the hall. Instantly Aleck sprang to barricade it with a stout oaken bar that stood beside it, saying as he did so, " I hear sounds at the rear of the house — we are fully surrounded -- we shall have to stand our ground."

The blazing fire on the hearth, seen through the crevices of the closed shutters, would reveal where the tenants of the house were, and hence, against the dining-room the attack was to be expected. Therefore, the entrance being barricaded, four distinct apertures were made in the clay-filling on its sides, near which the four defenders stationed themselves, to watch, and, if assaulted, to bring down the enemy. Mrs. Hawkins stood at the left of the door, where, if forced, it would first open, and her youngest son — still merely a boy of sixteen — was stationed beside her. The moon was at the full, but dense clouds obscured its light, casting a sort of spectral hue upon all surrounding objects. Soon every bush and sapling upon the lawn seemed to be in motion, and creeping slowly up the slope toward the devoted dwelling. Nearer they came, dim and shadowy, till they took the form of men — more than seventy in all, as this woman had the coolness to count in that perilous moment. Directly in her front, and not forty yards away, was a body of about twenty, huddled closely together, and bearing among them a felled tree, evidently to batter down the door of the dining-room. "Halt!" she cried, "Come one step nearer, and some of you are dead men."

No heed was given to her summons; the platoon moved forward a step or two, and then four rifles cracked, and five souls passed into eternity — two sent there by one bullet.

Then a yell went up that shook the hillside, and a volley poured into the beleaguered dwelling. All but one of the bullets buried themselves in the logs of the house — that one struck the clay-filling near the door-way, and entered the body of the boy who stood there beside his mother. He uttered a sudden cry, pressed his hand to his side, and sinking down at her feet, said only, "Oh, mother!"

She clutched him in her arms, tried to stanch the blood that spurted over her clothing, and then, bending her face down to his, kissed him upon the forehead, saying, "God is calling for you, my son! He is taking from me my baby."

"I know, mother," gasped the boy, "but I shall die like a man."

"Don't think of that, or of me now," she said, pressing her lips again to his forehead, "Think only of Jesus, the infinite Saviour."

"Yes, mother," faltered the boy, "Good bye — give the Rebels another shot, mother."

Then his head fell back, and he was gone from the sound of human conflict. She closed his eyes, and kissed again his forehead; then she rose to her feet, reloaded her rifle, and gave that other shot to the Rebels. Meanwhile the other young men had reloaded, and fired their guns, and the assaulting party had fallen back, evidently disconcerted by the determined resistance.

Half an hour followed during which the besieged neither saw nor heard any thing of their enemy, and they were beginning to think they had beaten them off, when suddenly the four corners of the roof above their heads were seen to be in a blaze. The building had been fired, and to this they could make no resistance. Nothing remained for the survivors but to run the gantlet of their enemies. Giving one look to her dead son, and one prayer to the God in whom she trusted, Mrs. Hawkins unbarred the door, and, followed by her two sons, sprang out into the darkness.

Dense shrubbery grew about the house, but it was fifty feet away, and before it could be reached the three would be a fair mark for more than sixty muskets. Mrs. Hawkins gained the shelter of the bushes in safety, but her two sons were shot down when not more than ten paces from the dwelling. "I saw them fall," she said to me, "and I knew there was no hope for them, for those men would have taken their lives, even if they had surrendered."

Shielded from sight by the shrubbery, she made her way to the barn, and once behind it, was safe in the darkness.

In fleeing thus from instant death, Mrs. Hawkins had merely obeyed the instinct of self-preservation; but that instinct momentarily appeased, her other faculties could assert themselves. But the mother-feeling was not the first to awake, bringing to her a full sense of her great bereavement, and her now absolute loneliness. It was her strong brain; and it now asked, "Why has the Lord taken them, who are men, and left me, who am only a woman, and can do so little for my country?" This, she told me, was her first thought, and the event was to her at first a mystery. "But afterward," she remarked, "I saw into His ways more clearly; and it is certain that the murder of my boys, who were beloved by everyone, did more than any thing else to convince the mountain people that death was better than life, when subject to the rule of such wretches as Colonel Keith. It shamed the timo-serving, and aroused the timid and lukewarm till they were eager to fight, and if need be, to die, for the Union. My manly boys were the sacrifice required to arouse a whole people to a full sense of their duty, and so, I bowed my head to the will of God. Ah! Sir, but it was a bitter struggle! Pray God you may never know such a heart-wrenching."

Protected by the darkness, Mrs. Hawkins made her slow way through the lately-fallen snow to a mountain-shelf, about a fourth of a mile from her dwelling. She was thinly clad, and it was one of the coldest nights in January, but there she paused to look back at her burning dwelling. She saw the flames leaping high above the roof, lapping up with remorseless greed her valued books, and the many other precious memorials of her dead husband. As this irretrievable loss occurred to her she felt a momentary pang; but soon she thought of the poor serving-woman, who, like herself, had been cast out upon the winter night, homeless, and with not so much as a temporary shelter. Doubtless she had escaped from the burning house, but what neighbor would face the wrath of Colonel Keith by giving a refuge to one of her family?

This thought troubled her as she stood there in the cold night, and watched — but scarcely heeded — the caving

19

in of the roof, the falling down of the walls, and the gradual sinking of the flames as they devoured all her earthly treasures. As she gazed she lived over again her life in that ruined dwelling — she recalled the eager zeal with which her husband and herself had entered upon their work among those mountain people; the sad day when she laid all that was mortal of him away in a lonely grave upon the hillside; the anxious care with which she had striven to guide aright the opening minds of her sons; the daily joy she had experienced when she saw them growing up manly, upright, God-fearing men, and the assured trust she had felt that they would be the stay of her declining years, and would at the last lay her tenderly away in that grass-grown grave by the side of her husband. All this came back to her as she stood there in the bitter night, homeless, childless, alone! But was she alone? Was not One with her who had Himself known every human sorrow? A voice within her seemed to whisper that He was, and sinking to her knees in the snow, she stretched out her arms to the clouded sky, and cried, "Dear Lord, be with me; sustain me; comfort me!" She had no sooner uttered the words than a strong light seemed to break around her, and she became so vividly conscious of an invisible, uplifting presence that all else appeared as nothingness; and rising above the loss of her home, and even of her children, she turned her back upon the burning pile, and strode forward into the snow-covered forest.

But now she began to be sensible to the cold which was striking upon her thinly-clad person, and chilling her through and through. She must find shelter, for weakened as she was by recent illness, she could not long survive if thus exposed till morning. She would gladly have died; but she had no right to die while her life could be preserved by any effort of her own — and the sense of right was the strongest element in her nature. So she strode forward through the forest, fully conscious that her every onward step was removing to a remoter day a joyful reunion with her husband and children.

At first she could call to mind no safe place of shelter; for in any of the neighbors' houses she would be exposed to capture by Colonel Keith and his soldiers. But soon it occurred to her that not far away, on the mountain-shelf where she was, stood a deserted cabin, to which no one ventured because it was thought to be haunted. The cabin had been the home of a worthless vagabond, who, along with his much-suffering wife, had suddenly disappeared a few years previous, leaving his few household possessions behind him. The general belief was that he had fled after committing a terrible crime, for directly after his absence became known, there began to issue from the house at night piercing cries and moans, as of a woman in distress. It was thought by these superstitious people that the woful sounds were from the spirit of the murdered wife, and, not even to secure the abandoned furniture, would they enter the deserted dwelling.

The house had, in truth, a spectral appearance. It was moss-grown, and fast falling to decay, and the spot whereon it stood was the wildest and dreariest of the entire mountain. A naked cliff, overtopping its very roof, rose directly in its rear, on one side was a grove of sombre hemlocks, and on the other, a ledge of perpendicular rock, skirting the margin of the rapid streamlet that flowed through the grounds of Mrs. Hawkins. The land in front, sloping down to the high-road, had once been cultivated, but now was overgrown with tangled thickets of laurel and ivy, which plainly told that the place had no human occupant.

The moon had struggled from behind the dense masses of gray cloud while Mrs. Hawkins was making her slow way through the forest, and it shone full and clear upon the deserted cabin when she waded through the deep drift that choked its open door-way. The one room had a cheerless and desolate aspect. In places the floor had rotted away, and everywhere it was strewn with decayed leaves blown in by the autumn winds. One of the windows was entirely open, and underneath it the snow had drifted, and it also lay several inches deep upon the broad hearthstone. Open as the cabin was it would afford only a wretched shelter, but behind the door, and shielded from the cold wind, was a straw bed, piled high with wolf and panther skins. Without attempting to close either door or window, Mrs. Hawkins removed her sodden shoes, crept into this bed, and buried herself deep under the thick skins with which it was covered.

After a time warmth returned to her chilled limbs, but she did not fall asleep, nor was she preternaturally wakeful. She had been like one who has received a sudden blow upon the head, which, while not depriving him of consciousness, forces his brain to intense, but abrupt and disjointed action. Now her mind had resumed somewhat of its natural balance, and she had begun to see things in their right relations, and to realize her utter loneliness, and the appalling bereavement that had befallen her. As she did so, intense gloom settled upon her spirit. She seemed to herself to be absolutely isolated from her kind — a solitary soul in a wide universe of darkness. And, as if in sympathy with the feeling within her, the world without became shrouded in a gloom that was simply and literally terrible. Thick clouds gathered again over the sky, shutting out moon and stars, and coming down in heavy flakes of snow which loaded all the atmosphere. Soon, too, a high wind arose, shaking the decayed logs of the ruined cabin, and screaming and howling through the forest like voices from some infernal realm of endless strife and disorder. As she listened she began to question if there is any light, or peace, or joy, or goodness, in all the wide creation. Is not this world, she thought, wholly given over to wickedness? Do not evil men — fiends in human shape — devoid alike of justice, mercy, and pity, rule and riot in it; and, if they rule in this world, do they not also in the other world, for thither evil men go, and can the mere laying off of the body change their natures? So, bad men become devils, and may it not be true that they return to earth, mingle again in human affairs and make their abodes in such desolate places as this lonely and blood-stained cabin?

While these thoughts were in her mind there came a sudden sound as of a heavy body falling upon the roof, followed by a sharp crash, and piercing cries that rent the outer air, and were answered by low moans, as of a woman in distress, coming from the opposite end of the room in which she was lying. Nothing she had ever heard was like these moans, so sepulchral were they, so unearthly, so diabolical. They must be, she thought, the utterance of demons, and in sudden terror, she raised herself upon her elbow, and prayed to the God who had never failed her. As she prayed her native courage came back, and, turning toward the corner whence the sounds proceeded, she said in a firm voice, "Whatever you are, spirit or devil, leave me — leave me alone with my sorrow." While she yet spoke the sharp cry rose again upon the outer air, and an answering moan came from within the apartment. Then a swift rush of feet sounded across the floor, and all again was silence.

She laid her head again upon her pillow of skins, uttered another prayer, and then, thoroughly exhausted with all she had undergone, she sank into a deep slumber. When she awoke the gray morning was streaming through the open door and window, and looking about the room, her attention was at once attracted to the huge fire-place now completely choked with snow. This explained the sudden crash upon the roof. A snow-slide from the overhanging ledge had fallen upon it, and entirely filled the chimney.

Then she rose, and, going to the door, she saw an explanation of the other ghostly phenomena in the track of some wild animal coming down the ledge, and in that of another issuing from the door-way of the cabin. She had intruded upon the lair of a brace of either wild cats or panthers. These were the only evil spirits which had disturbed her repose, but they were kinder than those in human form, for they had left her in peace — " alone with her sorrow." ·

CHAPTER IX.

A BURIAL BY TORCHLIGHT.

Whoever has suddenly lost a dear friend knows how hard it is, in the first days of bereavement, to realize that the lost one is dead; and he will remember that this is especially so, just after his awakening in the morning, when the mind — not yet in full possession of its scattered faculties, and moving in its accustomed groove — instinctively recalls the dead as still living, subject to the accidents of life, and claiming our wonted care and solicitude.

So it was with Mrs. Hawkins when she awoke in that desolate cabin, and looked out upon the dreary scene below her. Every object in field and forest was shrouded in a thick mantle of snow, except one solitary spot, where a heap of charred, and still smouldering logs, reminded her of the tragic events of the previous night. All the terrible tragedy then came back to her — the dying words of her youngest boy, the fall of her older sons; and she realized again that "there was no hope for them." Yet, she could not "make them dead." She fancied them still sensible to pain, still suffering from the bitter cold to which their bodies had been exposed through all the long hours of that winter night. Her first impulse was to hasten to their relief; and, wrapping about her a wolf-skin robe which she found in the deserted cabin, she set out through the drifts for her ruined home.

The snow had extinguished the flames, but the fire was still eating away at the logs, and sending out dense volumes of black smoke, which enveloped the ruins, and almost blinded her sight; but, groping about among the many drifts the wind had raised, she at last came upon two small heaps of snow under which lay the bodies of her older sons. Their faces were upturned to the morning light, and upon them both was an eager, expectant look, as if on their waning sight had risen a dim vision of the life hereafter. That look recalled her fully to herself, and made real to her, for the first time, that her boys were no longer sensible to cold, or pain, or any form of human suffering, except, it might be, grief at leaving their mother to meet alone the rude buffetings of this lower world.

She kneeled down, and kissed their cold lips; and then rose and went to the barn, which was still standing undisturbed — for the motive of the assailants had been murder, and not robbery, or wanton destruction. She did not seek for the body of her youngest son. As he had fallen while in the house, she knew that his remains lay under those burning logs, and, if ever recovered, would be merely a blackened mass, undistinguishable as a human form. The thought gave her a sudden pang, but it passed away when she reflected that her beloved boy was already clothed upon with a body from heaven, ethereal, resplendent, immortal.

At the barn the horse gave her his usual greeting; and when she patted him upon the neck, and spoke kindly to him, he responded with more than his accustomed cordiality. Doubtless, she was more than ordinarily gentle

20

with the animal, and he made only the natural return to her caresses; but still, she thought that he strove to make her feel that he sympathized with her distress. When one is suffering the loss of some human love, is there not a certain kind of solace in the affection of even a dumb creature? She waited for the horse to eat his morning provender, then, harnessing him to a sled, she lifted the bodies of her sons upon it, and conveyed them to the barn, where she laid them upon the floor, and covered them with blankets.

Removing then the harness, she put a saddle and bridle upon the animal, and, carefully fastening the barn, rode down the path to the highway. By this time a number of people — women and children, and a few old men — had collected about the ruins. They greeted her kindly and considerately; but asked no questions, and she made no remarks — they appeared to know already the whole horrid history. As she passed out of the gate-way, an aged woman who was coming up the road, paused directly in her path, and said to her, "Mornin', Mrs. Hawkins. Ye 'ortent ter be a ridin' off with nary kiver ter yer head. Tuck my bunnet. I wish ye wud, I've another ter home." With this she held out a thick quilted hood for Mrs. Hawkins's acceptance.

As she took it, she said, "Well, Betty, I will take it — the morning *is* cold."

She had been without any covering to her head since she had fled from her burning dwelling.

Her only thought now was to give the bodies of her two sons suitable interment. But who could she get to

dig their grave, and do the other offices of the sad cere-
mony? The miscreant Keith had hanged aged women
by the neck till they were nearly dead, for no other of-
fense than begging of him the bodies of their slaughtered
sons; and might he not do this by her, or even worse —
deprive her of liberty, and thus prevent her attending to
their burial? Evidently she must go forward with caution, for at any turn in the road she might come upon a
party of Keith's myrmidons. Then it occurred to her
that Sukey was competent to make all the necessary ar-
rangements, and could come and go without being molested. She would ride to the mill, and ask of her that
service in the emergency.

She had scarcely come to this resolution, when, looking
up the road, she saw, coming toward her, about twenty of
Keith's soldiers. They were riding rapidly, and would
very soon be abreast of her. There was no avoiding
them, so she rode forward, hoping that in her unusual
attire she could pass them without recognition. But
she forgot that her horse, if not her garments, would
identify her; and this the animal must have done, for before her features, hidden by her hood, were distinguish-
able, the squad halted in the highway. She felt sure of
being arrested, but she rode steadily forward.

The sergeant who has been already mentioned, was
at the head of the troop, and as she came near, he removed his cap, saying, " Pardon me, Mrs. Hawkins, if I
detain you long enough to say how deeply we sympathize
with you in your great affliction. We are the men who
were once quartered at your dwelling, and there is not

one of us who would not willingly give his own blood to bring your sons back to life. We all esteem you very highly."

"I thank you, Mr. Sergeant," she said. "I thank all of you — I feared you were about to arrest me, and that would have prevented my attending to the burial of my sons. Will you tell me if any orders are out to interfere with me?"

"I know of none," answered the sergeant, "and if any should be given, I think they would not be obeyed. There is a point beyond which a man will not go, orders or no orders. We have to report at once to head-quarters, or we would stay by, and protect you."

"I thank you, gentlemen," she said. "I cannot tell you the comfort your kind words give me. You have good hearts, if you do serve a bad cause; but that, I trust, will be forgiven you."

As she passed on all the men removed their caps, and they stood there uncovered till she was some distance down the high-road.

She was at the mill in less than an hour, and, going directly into the living apartments, found Sukey clearing away the breakfast table. Disguised as she was by her unwonted apparel, Sukey did not at once recognize her; as soon as she did, she exclaimed, "Why, Mrs. Hawkins! Ar' hit ye? Why, how pale an' porely ye luck, ma'am. Come, an' sit ye down by th' fire, and warm yerself. What has brung ye out uv so cold a mornin'?"

"Did you not see the fire on the mountain last night, Sukey?" asked Mrs. Hawkins.

"Yac, ma'am," said Sukey. "I seed hit, an' I won dered what pore man th' varmints was a burnin' out now."

"It was my home, Sukey, and I have come to ask you to help me about the burial of my sons."

"Yer sons, ma'am?" exclaimed Sukey. "Killed? Oh! doan't ye say hit — fur th' love uv th' good Lord, doan't ye say hit," and she sank into a chair, and looked appealingly at Mrs. Hawkins.

"I have to say it, Sukey dear," said Mrs. Hawkins, controlling herself by a strong effort. "They are all murdered."

"All!" echoed Sukey, swaying her body back and forth, and speaking in broken sentences. "Aleck, an' Benny, an' Billy-Boy — all! all! Them as I so loved — loike ez ef they was my own! All dead! killed — murdered!"

As she uttered the last word she sprang suddenly to her feet, and striding toward an inner door, exclaimed "An' *he* done hit! He shill answer fur hit." Saying this, she darted quickly from the room — too quickly for Mrs. Hawkins to have detained her, had that been her intention.

Sukey's manner was violent, and it boded harm to Justin; but the passage she had to traverse was long, and her good angel was with her on the way, for when she returned, her excitement had vanished, and her bearing was calm, though stern, and determined — something like that of a judge who, with no feeling for or against a criminal, is about to pass upon him an irrevocable sentence. Justin preceded her by a step or two in entering the apartment.

Mrs. Hawkins had removed her hood, and let the wolf-skin fall from her shoulders, and as she now sat by the fire, she was face to face with the Parson; but she gave him no sign of recognition. She looked at him, but did not appear to see him. He sank into a chair, his eyes riveted upon hers, and either the singularity of her manner, or some intuition of what was coming, drove the blood from his face, till its usual sallow hue was changed to a sickly pallor. Sukey was the first to speak. Standing directly in front of Justin, her features set as hard as flint, her great eyes glowing like burning coals, and looking him through and through, she said, "Robert Justin — der yer knows this lady?"

"I does, Sukey," he stammered, "Hit ar' Mrs. Hawkins."

"An' fur all uv twenty year she hev been dreffil good ter ye, haint she? — larned ye ter read, guv ye vittles an' clo'es when ye had nary, an' finerly got ye th' place in the meetin', so ye mout be as lazy ez ye loiked. Haint she done all this?"

"Yas, Sukey," he answered, taking his eyes from Mrs. Hawkins, and trembling visibly, "Mrs. Hawkins has done all thet — an' more'n thet."

"An' how has ye paid her?"

"I haint paid her," he stammered, "I doan't never 'spect I kin pay her."

"Ye lie, Robert Justin," said Sukey, in the same cold, flinty tone, her great eyes still blazing upon him, "Ye *has* paid her! Ye has sold her sons to Cunnel Keith. Fur a few dirty rags ez ye calls money, ye has murdered her boys — all she had in th' world."

He crouched down in his chair, covered his face with his hands, and moaned audibly. After a few moments, he said, "Oh! doan't ye say thet, Sukey—doan't ye say thet."

"I does say hit," said Sukey, "an' I say ter ye, too, thet in tuckin' them boys from thar mother, ye tuck them from me; an' they was loike they was my own. They and she was all I hed ter love in th' world. If she hadn't teached me better, I shud ax God now ter curse ye fur hit, an' He wud curse ye if I shud ax Him. But, I shan't. I leave Him ter do with ye as He loikes. Hit haint 'case I loathe ye thet fur more'n ten yere I haint been yer wife; but 'case th' little good thar's in me cudn't mate with th' evil thet's in ye. But I didn't know ye was so evil. I tho't ye mout be holped; but now, I see ye can't, an' I guv ye up. Go, put th' saddle on th' hoss, an' bring him ter th' door, while I gits my few things together. An' mind what I say, never agin do ye come whar I ar'—ef ye does, I won't be 'sponsible fur what'll happen."

The strongest element in this man's nature was love for that woman. Through long years he had hoped to win her back to him; and the thought that if his condition were bettered she might return to him, may have led him, for a filthy reward, to betray the Hawkins boys. Now he sat as one stunned, mumbling, "Why Sukey! ye won't leave me?"

She made him no reply, and then he turned to Mrs. Hawkins, "Ye doan't b'lieve, ma'am," he said, "thet I murdered yer boys?"

"I do not think you intended to murder them," she answered, scarcely looking at him. "I believe you betrayed them to Colonel Keith, and in your greed for the reward, you didn't stop to consider that in doing so you would cause their deaths. But you knew they would die rather than be captured. Their blood is on your hands, Robert Justin."

He covered his face again, and again moaned audibly. A few moments passed, no one speaking. Then Sukey said, in a husky, suppressed voice, "Robert Justin, thar's a devil ez is a tellin' me ye haint fit ter live, an' I orter to put ye out o' th' world. I've been a strugglin' agin him ever sence I know'd ye had killed th' boys; an' ef ye doan't git th' hoss an' let me go ter onct, he mout git th' upper hand uv me. So gwo ter onct—this instant."

Justin saw that she was dangerous, and, without a word, he rose and left the apartment.

Sukey had some thick garments which she wore only on special occasions, and in these she now insisted upon arraying Mrs. Hawkins. This done, and some few articles gathered into a small bundle, she led the way out to the high-road, where, at the hitching rail, stood her horse by the side of that of Mrs. Hawkins. Justin was not there nor, so far as I know, did Sukey ever meet him afterward.

As they rode on over the drifted snow Sukey said to Mrs. Hawkins, "I'se a thinkin' ma'am, 'bout th' burial of th' pore boys. Thar' haint nary uns 'cept old men round, and they'll be afeared ter holp ye, sence thet butcher, Keith, hev done sech things up ter Shelton Laurel.

But up ter the camp thar's more'n a hundred men, an' every one uv 'em wud die fur ye, if they know'd what's happened ter th' boys. 'Sides, they has looked fur Reuben ter be back 'fore now."

This suggestion commended itself to Mrs. Hawkins, and at once the two women rode forward to the camp of the refugees, which was high up on Spring Mountain, a few miles to the north of the Shelton Laurel. A heavy storm had again set in before they reached the base of the mountain, and by the time they began its ascent, the snow was falling so thickly that the path was completely hidden, and objects fifty yards distant, were only obscurely visible; but Sukey had been over the route on several occasions, and her familiar acquaintance with the forest enabled her to find their way without difficulty.

The camp consisted of about forty "half-faced cabins" — temporary structures formed by setting two upright poles, notched at the upper ends, firmly into the earth, and stretching a horizontal pole from one to the other, at about the height of a man's head, from which other poles sloped diagonally to the ground. Three sides of these cabins are usually covered with blankets or buffalo-robes, the front being left open; but often the four sides are inclosed, and then the cabin is a full protection against wind and weather.

The encampment of the refugees was approachable only over very steep and rugged ground, but the camp itself was on a level space, covered with gigantic oaks and poplars, and just at its rear, rising above the tops of these trees, was an abrupt ledge of rocks, accessible to

21

not more than half-a-dozen men at a time, and which a
hundred could hold against a thousand.   This was the
citadel of the encampment, to which it was intended that
the refugees should resort if assailed by greatly superior
numbers.

When the two women had arrived within about two hundred yards of this stronghold, they were hailed by a voice
from among the trees, with " Halt! who comes there?"

" Friends," answered Sukey, vainly trying to catch a
glimpse of the man through the thick-falling snow.

" Advance, friends, and give the countersign," responded
the voice.

" We uns'll advance," answered Sukey, " an' guv ye
th' countersign — ef ye'll tell us what hit ar'.   But you
uns needn't be afeard uv two wimmin — we wudn't do
ye a hurt fur th' world."

" We don't believe you would," said the voice, now
right at her elbow.   " What can have brought you out in
such a storm, Mrs. Justin?"

" Ter see th' cap'n," answered Sukey.   " Hev he got
back ter th' camp?"

" Yes, ma'am, not more'n an hour ago;" said the man,
" but he had a mighty narrow escape from Keith's men.
They knew he was coming, and set traps for him all
along the line.   Twelve of them surrounded him on the
Little Bald only the night before last; but he laid out
four or five, and put the rest to thar heels.   But, he'd have
been a dead captain, if it hadn't been for the three sixteen-shooters he was bringing along for the Hawkins
boys.   He's all worn out, but he'll see *you*."

The cabin of Ellis was somewhat larger, and better furnished, than the others. In one corner was a bed, supported on a frame of saplings, in another, a rude table, and scattered about the ground — which was covered with deer and bear skins — were a number of rustic seats, fashioned like camp-stools. On a rack against the rear wall were four sixteen-shooting Henry carbines, three of them evidently new, but already smeared with gunpowder. On the table were some plates, and broken food, the remains of Ellis's breakfast.

He was resting upon the bed, when, unannounced, Mrs. Hawkins entered the cabin. Springing at once to his feet, he grasped her by the hand, saying, "I am so glad to see you. But what brings you here in this storm? And the boys — the men tell me they have been away nearly three days. I hope nothing has happened to them."

"They are dead, Reuben," she answered, slowly and deliberately. "They are all dead."

He staggered back a step or two, put his hand to his forehead, and exclaimed, "Dead! It can't be true! All dead?"

"It *is* true, Reuben," she said, in the same subdued tone. "They are all dead — shot down before my very eyes."

As now he looked at her his eyes seemed starting from their sockets, his great chest heaved, and clasping his two hands above his head, he cried out, each separate word a distinct utterance of agony. "My God! — my God! — Dead! The boys dead, and I alive to hear it!"

Then he sank upon one of the stools, and looked out

with a fixed, vacant stare upon the falling snow. But he seemed to see nothing — to be unconscious of even her presence. While one might count a hundred he sat thus — lost, dazed, bewildered. Then he rose to his feet, and taking both her hands in his, he said to her with a look of unutterable tenderness, "And *you* to be so afflicted — *you* whose whole life has been given to others, who have been so good to me, to all — *you* to be left alone, with no one to love or to care for you ! Oh, madam ! Let me love you — let me watch over you, let me be your son, let Phebe be your daughter, let our little boys be your children, till you go to your own noble boys in a better world than this is." With his last words a great cry broke from her, and throwing her arms about his neck, she sank weeping upon his breast.

My summer home is where I look down upon a beautiful lake ; and, going there in a backward Spring, I often see it entirely overspread with sheeted ice. Thus it has been before the sun has risen much above the opposite mountains, but when scarcely an hour has passed, and the warm rays have come down in their full power, I have seen the ice suddenly sink into the bosom of the lake, leaving it a broad expanse of glistening water reflecting the warm sun and the blue sky above. So was it with Mrs. Hawkins. The icy self-restraint in which she had been held, melted suddenly away in the warmth of this man's unselfish affection, and once more her soul opened itself to the sunshine of human sympathy and human love. Until this moment she had not shed a tear, but now the waters were unbound, and she wept unrestrainedly.

She sank upon one of the rude stools, and Reuben sat down by her side, holding her hand in silence. Sukey, meanwhile, had stood by with streaming eyes, but now, falling on her knees at Mrs. Hawkins's feet, she threw her arms about her, and exclaimed, " An' I will love ye, ma'am. I'se allers loved ye; but now I'll wuck fur ye, I'll live fur ye, I'll die fur ye — an' I'll never leave ye."

" And you shall not live any longer in this constant fear," said Reuben. " I'll take you, and Phebe and the children, and Sukey, too, if she'll go, and at the North we'll live in peace together."

Now, for the first time, Mrs. Hawkins found her utterance. "Oh, no! dear Reuben," she said, " we won't do that. Our duty is here. Here you can do more than you could possibly do in the North. But, the loving words of both of you are an inexpressible comfort to me. God is very good to give me two such true hearts as yours."

The storm continued, but soon trusty men were mounted upon the half-dozen horses that were in the encampment, and dispatched in various directions, to ascertain the exact position of Keith's forces. Before many hours they all returned, reporting that each separate squad within a radius of five miles of the Hawkins plantation, had been seen by the country people, early that morning, moving in the direction of Keith's head-quarters. This indicated that the Confederate commander was concentrating his men, either to attack the refugees in their camp, or to move his entire force to the more easterly counties.

Whichever course he might pursue, Ellis decided to break camp, and march with all his men to the Hawkins homestead. Keith outnumbered him four to one, but every one of his men was inflamed to fury by the slaughter of the Hawkins boys, and willing to risk his life in giving them suitable burial. Taking account of the spirit of the refugees, the strength of the opposing forces was therefore not so very unequal.

They began their march about an hour before sunset. The snow was no longer falling, but it lay a foot in depth upon the ground, and the lowering sky presaged another storm, with a night of intense darkness; but the men pressed on over the sharp rocks, and untrodden snow, as eagerly as if they had been bound to a wedding, rather than a burial, and a possible encounter with largely superior numbers. Because of her knowledge of the route, Sukey, with a couple of mounted men, led the way; directly behind her rode Mrs. Hawkins and Ellis, and then followed the main body, marching four abreast, with flankers, and a rear-guard. No attack was expected on the route, nor before the men had arrived at the homestead, and the burial was over; but strict silence was enjoined, and the pine torches the men carried were not ignited.

About an hour after sunset the troop wound up the steep road that led to the burned dwelling. The snow had completely extinguished the fire, and the whole mountainside was now shrouded in thick darkness. The few among the men who were mounted, being sent up and down the road to give warning of any hostile approach, the remainder lighted their torches, and set to work to

remove the half-burned logs that had fallen into the cellar
of the ruined dwelling; for Mrs. Hawkins had expressed
a wish to have the bodies of her sons buried together, and
the remains of her youngest were somewhere underneath
those blackened timbers.

While the larger number were thus employed, the few
carpenters who were in the troop were engaged in con-
structing coffins for the older sons from the boards of a
feed-bin at the barn. Sukey remained at the barn with
these carpenters, but Mrs. Hawkins sat her horse beside the ruins, watching with eager eyes each charred log
as it was lifted from the choked-up cellar. At last when
every timber had been removed, and nothing found bearing even a faint resemblance to a human form, a dozen
torches were lowered into the vault, and every heap of
cinders was closely examined. Still, nothing was discovered that could be identified as the remains of the brave
boy, but recently so keenly alive with youth, and hope,
and manly ambition. When all search was found to be
vain, Mrs. Hawkins said to Ellis, "The body of my baby
boy is here, Reuben, and I want my sons buried together.
Let us lay them all here — let their old home be their
grave."

It was done as she suggested. On a designated spot in
the vault a crib was made by placing the larger and
sounder logs one upon another in the form of a square;
and into this square were then lowered the coffins of the
older brothers. Then, at a signal given by Ellis, all
the men gathered around the vault, forming a circle of
which he and Mrs. Hawkins were the centre. Every

third or fourth man held a torch above his head, and the combined flames shed a lurid glare over the blackened ruin, the white, drifted snow, and the stern, sad faces of the stalwart men, who, at the hazard of their lives, had come to render the last earthly service to their murdered comrades. When all were in their places, their rifles ready to meet any sudden assault, Mrs. Hawkins, throwing back her hood, so that her features were distinctly visible, spoke to them somewhat as follows:

"I can hardly find words, dear friends, in this terrible hour, to thank you for the kindly aid you have given me, at so much risk to yourselves. My mother-heart is too stricken for speech; and yet, if the death of my true, brave sons shall aid in freeing our country from its great sin, I shall fold my hands, and try to say, 'God's will be done.' If their example shall inspire one soul to do right, and to lead a better and nobler life, they will not have died in vain; and when your children's children shall sit in peace and freedom around their happy firesides, will they not thank God that such men have lived and died to give them a purer and better country? Pray, dear neighbors and friends, not for my sons — they need no one's prayers — but pray for their desolate mother, that she may be able to say from her heart, 'God's will be done.'"

Here a great sob choked her utterance. She could say no more, and taking her horse by the bridle, Ellis led her away to the barn. The men continued to pile the logs one upon another till they had risen to a considerable height from the ground, and this being done, all marched back unmolested to the camp upon the mountain.

The pile of logs, all charred and furrowed as when fresh from the fire, still rose upon the spot when Mrs. Hawkins related to me these incidents; and as she finished the narration, she led me to the door-way of her dwelling, and, pointing to the pile, said, " There, Sir, is where I buried my boys, on the spot where they were born, the ruins of our old home for their monument; and down there, Sir, by the spring, is where twenty misguided men gave up their lives for the crime Colonel Keith had committed."

22

CHAPTER X.

SUKEY AS A SCHOOL-MISTRESS.

SENDING scouts out on the following morning, Reuben Ellis speedily discovered why he had not been molested at the burial of the sons of Mrs. Hawkins. Soon after noon of that day Keith had withdrawn his entire regiment from the county, to carry fire and musket-ball into some other unhappy district of the mountains. Being thus freed from any possible interruption, Ellis proceeded at once to rebuild the burned dwelling, meanwhile relinquishing to Mrs. Hawkins and Sukey, his own half-faced cabin on Spring Mountain.

The new house in external appearance was, as nearly as possible, a duplicate of the old one ; and it was located on the same outlying knoll of the mountain, where from its windows, the desolate mother could look out upon the grave of her slaughtered sons. In internal fitting-up, however, it was totally different. The antique furniture and priceless mementoes of Benjamin Hawkins, were replaced by rustic chairs, lounges, and sideboards — the handiwork of the deft mountaineers — and by numerous articles from the " best-rooms " of the neighboring population, which had been forced upon Mrs. Hawkins. Indeed, so general was the sympathy with the bereaved woman that, before her house was fully completed, she was obliged to send back to its owners a large portion of the " store-

bought" furniture of that mountain region. Not till the
dwelling was entirely finished and furnished, and Mrs.
Hawkins, with Sukey and Martha, had moved into it, did
Reuben Ellis set out with the refugees on the long tramp
into Tennessee.

Ellis had scarcely left the district before another Confederate regiment appeared in the neighborhood. It came
upon the same errand as the preceding one, but, either
the Confederate authorities had been shocked by the
atrocities of Keith, or its commander, General Alfred E.
Jackson, was a man of some humanity. He certainly did
not proceed on the supposition that the indiscriminate
killing of all the able-bodied men in the community would
enable it to furnish the Confederacy with the requisite supply of soldiers. Only one life was taken by Jackson's
troops, still, his occupation of the district was attended
with barbarities that cannot be glossed over in any faithful picture of the war in this region.

"When Jackson arrived," says Daniel Ellis, "he ordered
eight or ten families to be moved into one house, and in
this way he had nearly all the houses vacated, with the
exception of the few which contained the women and
children, and these he had closely guarded. He ordered
all the vacant houses to be burned to ashes, and he also
gave orders for all the stock in the country to be destroyed.
He adopted this method, he said, in order to starve the
Union men out of the mountains, so that they would be
compelled to come in, and join the Confederate army.
It was now February, the snow was deep, and the weather
was extremely cold."

" The Rebel soldiers would build up large fires out of
fence-rails, and lay around them, while the shivering
women and children were not permitted to have any fire at
all.   Sometimes the little children would go to the fires
where the Rebel soldiers were, to warm their aching hands
and feet; the Rebels would then compel them to stand so
close to the burning flames that the little innocent creatures
would scream out in severe agony of suffering; and when
their mothers would approach to rescue them, the Rebels
would present their pistols, and tell them, if they attempted
to relieve their children, they would blow a ball through
them.   *   *   The women and children suffered greatly
for something to eat, for the Rebels devoured all their
provisions.   Very frequently it occurred, that, for a whole
day together, they could not obtain any thing at all.   This
gang of Rebel soldiers remained in this neighborhood for
eighteen or twenty days, and then returned to Greenville,"
Tennessee.

But this savage desolation of an entire district did not
add a single recruit to the army of the Confederacy.
From their hiding-places in the mountains the men of the
region beheld their homes razed to the ground, and their
wives and children driven forth without food or shelter;
but they preferred to see their nearest kindred suffer, and
to themselves perish — as some of them did — of cold
and starvation, rather than lift their hands against their
country.   But, since the world began it has never been
known that the one who set duty above life, was utterly
forsaken.   This fact was noticed by David, and has been
also by every other man who has attentively observed

the world around him, or looked closely into history. And how can it be otherwise, when, in the very nature of things, all the good forces of the universe are on the side of him who persistently follows truth and justice.

But strength is born of weakness, and so relief came to this distressed people from the sorely-stricken woman, who, in her desolate home, sat now, hour after hour, looking out upon the heap of charred logs that covered all that had held her to this human life we are living. Her house and her horses and cattle had been spared, and not even a solitary soldier had so much as intruded upon her premises. This may have been because she had now no sons liable to conscription, or for the reason that the great calamity which had befallen her, had invested her with a kind of sacredness in the eyes of even her enemies. Whichever it was, her barn was unmolested, though filled to the eaves with a generous harvest. At the very first entrance of Jackson into the district she had heard of the rapacity of his soldiery, and before two days had fully passed she saw from her windows the homes of her humble neighbors going up in flames. Then she said to Sukey, "We have plenty, and those people will soon be starving; but how can we get any thing to them? If we send them corn, and the soldiers know it, they will come and destroy our every bushel."

"I've been a thinking of that, ma'am," said Sukey. "Thar 'pears ter me only one way; but I'se afeard hit mout be too hard upon ye, ma'am."

"And what is the way?" asked Mrs. Hawkins.

"'Ter open the schule agin, ma'am, an' put th' corn in th' young uns bags when they goes home. Ter make hit light fur ye, I'll larn th' children, an' ye shill only look on an' see I does hit right."

Sukey "larnin'" the children! Sukey a school-mistress! The thought was so very absurd that Mrs. Hawkins had to smile, but she said nothing. However, Sukey's quick intelligence detected her thought, and answering it she said, "Hit won't make any difference, ma'am; fur th' chillen won't come fur larnin'; they'll come fur corn."

" So they will, Sukey," said Mrs. Hawkins, now laughing outright — the first laugh that had brightened her features since the death of her sons. " Come here and kiss me, Sukey." Then as Sukey put her arms about her, she added, "you are a dear, good soul, Sukey. The Lord is very kind to give you to me. You *shall* teach the children—for I haven't the strength—and teaching them, you will learn yourself."

It was not half an hour before Sukey, mounted on the back of Sam, was on her way to every house where the burned-out people had been gathered, to invite all the children to the school which Mrs. Hawkins had decided to again open at her dwelling, and to say, in a quiet aside to the mothers, "see thet th' young uns is bundled up warm in a shawl, or a blanket, big 'nuff ter hide a small bag uv corn; an' mind thet nary one uv th' sogers sots eyes on hit — 'case ef he do, he'll come an' stole our fodder, an' ye mout git no more uv hit."

So, the school opened with Mrs. Sukey Justin as school-mistress, and never was school so well attended in any

region not subject to compulsory education. Far and
wide the news spread, till all the young folks for many
miles around showed a greed for learning never before
witnessed in that community. When, on only the second
day of the school, the children were seen to come from
long distances, Sukey said to Mrs. Hawkins, "With th'
snow up ter thar knees, ma'am, haint hit fearsome bad for
th' young uns ter foot hit both ways, an' tote th' corn
besides. Won't ye let me hitch th' two nags ter th' big
sled, an' tote 'em home in th' hay-rick?"

And thus, while suffering and sorrow brooded over
every household in the scattered community, there was
daily joy among not less than forty of those mountain
children. Even the sore heart of Mrs. Hawkins forgot its
pain, when she saw the gleeful little ones pile,. thick as
sardines in a box, among the straw at the bottom of the
sled, and heard the woods ring with their unrestrainable
shouts and laughter. At such times Sukey would say to
her, with glad tears in her eyes, "Hit does me good, ma'am,
ter see ye enjoy hit. Thar's a blessin' on ye in th' hearts
uv every one uv these young uns, an' hit will holp th'
good Lord ter lift th' burden frum ye — I knows hit
will." ·

Then Sukey would cry "G'lang" to the horses, and
down the hill they would go like shot from a musket-bar-
rel, the children screaming with delight, and Mrs. Hawkins calling from the door-way, "Not so fast, Sukey, you'll
land them in a snow-bank." "Never mind ef I does,"
Sukey would shout back, "Hit'll do 'em good;" and
then, making carefully the turn at the foot of the hill,

she would shout again, "G'lang" to the horses, and away
they would plunge through the snow, waking the echoes
of the quiet hills, and sending at least a momentary joy
through those terror-stricken mountains. Even the soldiers would cheer them as they swept by, and — good-
feeling being contagious — these daily merry-makings no
doubt served to relax the rigor of their watch upon the
crowded households. It is certain that, though the bags
were often exposed to their sight, and frequently were
large enough to supply the outlying men in the mountains,
the sentries never once looked under the straw in the sled,
nor cast a suspicious glance upon Mrs. Hawkins's gran-
ary. There were isolated cases of cruelty on both sides
during the war, but its whole history shows that the same
human heart beat under the gray coat that beat under the
blue.

After a brief time Jackson's soldiers disappeared from
the neighborhood, and then the necessity which had
called the school into being no longer existed; but the
daily sessions were continued. Sukey saw that with so
much young life about her, Mrs. Hawkins was being
gradually drawn away from her sorrow, and from the
unworldliness in which she had been fast losing all interest in mere human affairs. To Sukey's untutored intel-
lect this had not seemed a natural condition. As she read
the earthly career of the Great Master she discerned that
He had touched our human life at its every point — had
wept with its sorrows, taken pleasure in its innocent en-
joyments — all the while that His soul had been infused
with the diviner life of a higher world. We should, she

thought, live as He lived, and hence, it was with great
gladness that she now saw Mrs. Hawkins emerging from
her icy isolation, and sympathizing again with the joys
and sorrows of the human life around her.

And I may as well say here that Sukey was a decided
success as a school-mistress. Illiterate and ignorant as she
was, she had in her heart the impelling motive of all
great achievement — love, grateful love to the pure soul
who had led her out of darkness into Christ's own marvelous light. So with all her heart she bent her mind to
interesting Mrs. Hawkins in this new work. She could
write reasonably well, read fluently, and spell — when
the book was before her; but her real strength lay in
arousing the minds of her scholars, and exciting their
ambition. Her methods were unique, as were the circumstances under which she labored. There was not a spelling-book, a reader, or an arithmetic, in the entire community, for in the years it had been without a school such
things had gone to kindle the fires, or been swept out of
doors with the rubbish. She had only her Bible, and a
few newspapers that she had begged of Jackson's soldiers.
But with these as her text-books, she taught the children
their letters, then how to spell, and to read; first having
them repeat the lesson orally after her, and then, to come
up to her table, and pick out the words, or the sentences,
for themselves from her Bible. And in numberless ways,
and with infinite tact, she excited in them emulation, and
lured them on to higher attainment.

All this, with her sewing or knitting in her hand, Mrs.
Hawkins observed from her arm-chair in the corner of the

23

huge fire-place, at first with an amused, but absent, curiosity; then with more active interest; and at length with genuine admiration.   Then one day when the lessons had been recited somewhat sooner than usual, she said to Sukey, "Let me tell the children a little story:" and she told them of David and Goliath — how the little stripling had overcome the great giant — the moral of which was that however young and feeble a child was, he would, if armed with truth and right, be strong enough to conquer the most formidable obstacles.

The children listened to the story with wondering delight, and, as school was about to close on the following day, one of the little fellows spoke up timidly, and said, "Please, ma'am, won't ye tole we uns another uv them powerful nice stories."   So, she told them another, and another, till every day a Bible story wound up the school exercises; and, after a time, she said to Sukey, "Don't you think, Sukey, that the school has grown too large for you to manage alone — had I not better take the older children, and you the younger?"   This she did, becoming day by day more interested in the work, till, after another while, she spoke again.   "The children," she said, "like my stories so much that I've been thinking their mothers might like them, too.   Suppose, Sukey, that we call them together here on Sundays, and read and talk to them.   If it should do them no other good, it will take their minds off from thinking of their husbands, and their own desolate condition."

The mothers came, bringing their children with them, and the house was filled to overflowing.   First, Mrs.

Hawkins made a prayer, and they sang together; and then she read from the Scriptures, making such simple explanations as were adapted to their capacities, and asking them to question her about any portion that they did not understand. Then again they prayed and sang together, and then the women went away, but not till they had all gathered about Mrs. Hawkins, and told her that she had been an angel of mercy to them all through that terrible winter, and that she had always been so; that they had nothing to give her in return, except their love, but God would reward her. They made no allusion to her lost sons, but the quivering lips, the tearful eyes, the sympathetic tones, of every one of them told that they felt, what they did not utter, lest it should open afresh the wound which had already bled too freely.

When the last one had gone away Mrs. Hawkins clasped her arms about Sukey, and in a broken voice said, "Oh! Sukey, I have been so selfish! I have thought only of my own sorrow, while so many distressed people have been all around me." Thus it was that she came back to herself — was born anew into this every-day world ; and thereafter she daily found a deeper and a holier life in giving of her own life and light to others.

That night, when Sukey went to her bed, she fell upon her knees, and thanked the good Lord for enabling her to lead the one she so much loved back to the sunshine of human joy, and to the blessedness of active work for others. For she knew that *she* had done this. And this is the miracle of human love. God pity the man or the woman who has to go through this world without it.

No sooner had the last of Jackson's troops left the district than the outlying mountaineers emerged from their hiding-places to rebuild their ruined dwellings. Placing sentries on the roads leading to Warm Springs and Marshall, and working in a single, well-armed gang of about fifty, they incurred but little risk of interruption, and it was not long before all the burned-out families were again sheltered in their own domiciles. Therefore, about the sole result of Jackson's raid had been to give each of the mountaineers a new house for an old one.

The only concern now experienced by the neighborhood was a threatened shortage of provisions. Jackson's soldiers had not only lavishly consumed, they had wantonly destroyed, both corn and cattle ; and in feeding the entire community the store of Mrs. Hawkins would be exhausted long before harvest. In these circumstances it was unexpectedly discovered that these distressed people had been unwittingly storing up provision for precisely such an emergency. Sukey had been uniformly reticent as to her reasons for sundering her relations with Justin, but now she let a few of her intimates understand that he was a thief — and that the avails of his systematic pilfering were at that very time stored away, in capacious bags, in the loft of the mill.

The mountaineers were learned enough in the law to know that one has a right to recover his own wheresoever he may find it ; but it is doubtful if they paused to debate the legality of the proceeding ; for without delay they descended upon the mill, thrust Justin and his assistant into a couple of dark closets, and then removed the

stolen grain to their own dwellings. Thus, by simply
reclaiming their own, they were amply provisioned till
another harvest. Of course, Justin denied the taking of
any more toll than custom and law allowed him, but this
statement had but little weight with a jury of hungry
stomachs.

As was natural, this disclosure of Justin's real character
led to his being ostracized by the entire mountain community. Men turned their faces away if they met him
in the road, and, rather than send grist to his mill, women
converted their corn into meal by the primitive process of
pounding. With no grist to grind the great wheel ceased
rotating, the dubious assistant absented himself from the
district, and Justin went into winter quarters, hibernating
upon gloomy reflections, and such sweepings of the mill
as had escaped the eyes of his neighbors. Relieved thus
from espionage, the community resumed much of its
normal existence, the only indication of apprehended
danger being the piles of brush, which, every here and
there, were in readiness along the high-roads, to give warning of the approach of any body of soldiery.

The deep snow upon the mountains soon forced Reuben
Ellis to suspend his trips into Tennessee; but fugitives —
now mostly escaped prisoners of war — continuing to
come in, they were quartered about in the various cabins
and barns in the neighborhood, at least a dozen having
lodgings in the hay-loft of Mrs. Hawkins. After a time
the number of fugitives became so large that it was evident the supply of corn would be exhausted before another harvest, and then Reuben Ellis set out through

the snow for the vicinity of Morganton, to divert the tide to a loyal district on the borders of Wilkes county, where they would find a cordial welcome and provisions in abundance. With the exception of this brief absence, he remained at home during all of this winter after February, going about the neighborhood much as usual, and with his wife making frequent visits to Mrs. Hawkins, with whom he had left his older boy to "keep her company," and have the advantage of Sukey's "tuition." It was not till early in April that the melting of the snow made it practicable for him to lead the large number of escaped prisoners, who, by that time, were quartered on the district, through the mountains into Tennessee.

He had made two or three subsequent trips, when one night late in July, he came to the dwelling of Mrs. Hawkins. After her usual kindly greeting she said to him, "It is long since I saw you in such exuberant spirits, Reuben — you have good news to tell me."

"I have, ma'am," he answered, seating himself, and taking his little boy upon his knee; "the Federals have made a strong raid around Knoxville, and Daniel Ellis says it is a reconnoissance, with a view to retaking Cumberland Gap, and occupying East Tennessee. I have no doubt he knows, for he is in the confidence of the Union generals."

"The Lord be thanked!" exclaimed the lady. "We have waited long, but I knew that deliverance would come. With a Union force in Tennessee, you can stand your ground, and drive such miscreants as Keith out of the mountains."

"I could have done that before now, ma'am," answered Reuben, "if you had not objected. Two or three times Keith has been within reach of my carbine. It astonishes me that you feel no bitterness toward that man."

"Should I be angry with the rod that has smitten me? Did not the Lord say to Pilate, 'You could have no power over me except it were given you from above?' Keith has been merely His instrument — it has been the Lord's doings, and, therefore, I submit."

"It is wonderful to me that you can," he answered. "I have had no wrongs like yours, and yet, I can't help hating every Rebel of them all; and as for Keith, I would as soon kill him as I would a rattlesnake."

"He has much the nature of one," said Mrs. Hawkins, "but such men are found everywhere. Times like these bring them to the surface, to the disgrace of both sides, and we should not charge their acts upon the Southern people who are just as good and conscientious as we are. They merely hold wrong opinions. It is their leaders who are besotted with either folly or wickedness."

"Then you think we can soon stand our ground with safety?" said Ellis.

"I do, as soon as there is a Union force in Tennessee, that you can fall back upon in case of defeat. You can collect the men who are lying out in the mountains, and with them, and such escaped prisoners as may be willing to remain here and fight for us, you can overcome any force the Confederates can afford to send against us. While we are surrounded on all sides, it is folly to resist; and the wisest course is to get our men through to the Union armies. But, the moment that the blood shed will not be wasted, then, drive every Rebel from the mountains. They are ours, and we have a right to our own firesides."

"And, after two years of almost uninterrupted defeat, are you still confident that the Union cause will be finally successful?" asked Ellis.

"Most certainly I am," answered Mrs. Hawkins. "We suffered defeat so long as Mr. Lincoln was willing to save the Union with slavery; but the moment he decided to issue his Emancipation Proclamation the tide began to turn. This convinces me that God intends the extirpation of slavery. The country may have to wade through even deeper seas of blood; but freedom will come at last, and then we shall have a great and united nation.

CHAPTER XI.

MORE HOUSE BURNING.

EARLY in September, 1863, came tidings to these belea-guered people that Cumberland Gap had been recaptured by the Union troops, and that Colonel Foster, with the advance of Burnside's army, had occupied Knoxville. Bragg was concentrating his forces at Chattanooga, but Rose-crans was moving against him; and thus did the great valley between the Alleghany and Cumberland Mountains, of which Knoxville is the centre, seem about to be permanently delivered from the control of the Confederates. The Union advance was everywhere received with a joy that had no bounds. "Everywhere," says an eye-witness, "the people flocked to the roadsides, and, with cheers and wildest demonstrations of welcome, saluted the flag of the Republic, and the men who had borne it in triumph to the very heart of the Confederacy. Old men wept at the sight, which they had waited for through months of sufferings; even children hailed with joy the sign of deliverance. Nobly had these persecuted people stood by their faith."

The news had been sent back to Mrs. Hawkins by a special messenger from Reuben Ellis, at Elizabethton; and he wrote that he was about to go forward to the head-quarters of the Union commander, to secure from him the detail of an officer competent to drill and lead troops,

24

together with a small squad of regular soldiers, around
whom the mountain men might rally, and permanently
hold Madison county. He added that he would himself
be at home within a fortnight. The returned refugee
who brought this letter from Ellis, said that he had come
by the way of the camp on Spring Mountain, where
Squire Plotts had just arrived, with a party of thirty
fugitives from Haywood county, who had come on to be
guided through the mountains. At once Mrs. Hawkins
loaded a couple of horses with provisions, and dispatched
them by Sukey to Squire Plotts, together with a letter,
giving him the news from Ellis, and advising that the
men should wait his return from Tennessee.

These tidings spread universal joy through all the
mountain region; but the rejoicing was of short duration,
for soon again did the red hand of war press heavily upon
the devoted community. Driven back by the advance of
the Union forces, Colonel Keith had decamped from
Tennessee, and again made his appearance in Madison
county. And again was his way marked by burning and
bloodshed. His regiment, says Daniel Ellis, "visited
Shelton Laurel, and burned a number of houses belonging
to Union men, and then murdered John Metcalfe by
shooting him in the head, and running their bayonets
through him six times. They also murdered Robert
Hare by shooting him three times. Their next victim was
Marion Franklin. He was ploughing in the field, perfectly
unconscious of his dreadful doom, when one of the Rebel
outlaws walked up to the fence, and shot him in the hip.
When the ball struck him he ran to a large stump which

was surrounded with bushes, and laid down; there he remained for a short time, writhing and groaning with severe agony, until his murderers came up, and relieved him from his misery by shooting him in the breast."

"The infamous murderers went coolly and calmly along in their horrible work of destruction and death. The next victims who had the misfortune of falling into their hands were Tilman Landers, Absalom Brucks, and a little boy, all of whom were caught at Mrs. Ruth Shelton's stable, and unceremoniously murdered on the spot. They caught David Shelton at his house, hung him until he was dead, and then dragged him to a laurel thicket, where they covered him with leaves. A few women afterward removed his body, and gave it a more humane burial." Having committed these atrocities, Colonel Keith took up his quarters on Rich Mountain, which indicated that he had discovered that the refugee encampment was not more than a mile away, upon the adjoining mountain.

Scarcely more than an hour after this significant movement became known to Mrs. Hawkins, the Confederate sergeant, who has been already mentioned, rode up to her door-way with a squad of about twenty soldiers. Dismounting, he asked to see Mrs. Hawkins, and, the school being in session, Sukey conducted him into the dining-room. As Mrs. Hawkins entered the room he removed his cap, and bowing low, said to her, "I have often to do unpleasant duties, madam; but I never did one so unpleasant as now — I am ordered to burn your dwelling."

"Then," said the lady, without the slightest exhibition of surprise or indignation, "not content with having murdered my sons, Colonel Keith would now deprive me of shelter?"

"He intends you no bodily harm, madam," answered the sergeant, "or he would not have sent *me* on this errand. He means to drive you from this neighborhood — he thinks it altogether owing to you that he can get no recruits in the mountains."

"He may be partly right," she replied, "but he doesn't help himself by burning my house. The mountain people make my cause their own, and they will be only the more embittered against him by this new vandalism. It has been solely out of regard to my wishes, that they have till now spared his life; and on several occasions he has been within reach of their rifles. But now, let him look to himself, for at his every step in these mountains he will be in danger. Please say this to him, and that only by taking my life can he drive me away from my home."

"I shall have to soften what you say, madam," answered the sergeant, "for Colonel Keith is a very passionate man, and he might do you actual violence. At times he seems possessed of a devil."

"I have no doubt he is," rejoined Mrs. Hawkins; "but do not soften a word I have said; and say also that if he stays in this neighborhood another fortnight he will be exterminated. We shall by that time have men enough to annihilate his regiment. The tables have turned, and these mountains are to be free. Soon Colonel Keith will be the hunted, not the hunter."

"He ar' a devil," now said Sukey; "but yer' a decent

young man — only ye hev ter obey orders. But ye haint nary orders to burn th' barn an' th' fixin's in th' house?"

"Nothing was mentioned except the house, Mrs. Justin," answered the sergeant; "but I suppose it is intended we shall burn every thing."

"Well, suppose ye foller th' letter uv th' law," said Sukey, "and let us save th' house fixin's. Ye see, thar's plenty of logs kin be got from th' woods, but if ye burn th' rest, hit's 'bout all thar is in Madison county."

"Let me speak to my men about it," said the sergeant, "if they consent, we'll not burn the barn, and will help you to remove the furniture."

As he went out to consult his men, Mrs. Hawkins said to Sukey, "I never should have thought of that. Sukey— you are a treasure."

In a few moments the sergeant reappeared at the door, with a gratified look upon his face. "The men consent," he said, "but we must be quick about it, or we shall be called to account for our delay."

Going then to the door, Sukey said to the dozen soldiers who composed the squad, "Ye ar' decent men, ebery one uv ye, ef ye is Rebels. Ef ye ever repent uv that, ye kin come hyar, an' hev a small fairm, an' a right nice gal ter marry ye. Now, we'll git th' things ter th' barn. I'll ax ye ter tuck th' heavy ones, while the chil'ren tote the little fixin's, an' I screw off th' doors an' winders — ye see we couldn't git nary more uv them in all these mountains."

In but little more than half an hour there was nothing left of the house but its log walls, and puncheon flooring.

Fire was then set to a pile of brush in the sitting-room, and soon it flamed above the roof, to tell Colonel Keith, at his camp six miles away, that his brutal order had been executed. Then Snkey said to the men, "Ye has wucked well, an' now I want ye ter taste of my apple-jack — hit's uv my own makin'."

While the men were imbibing the exhilarating fluid, Sukey said to them, "We shill hev th' house up agin by ter morrer, or next day; an' ef th' cunnel orders hit down agin, jist ye ax ter do th' burnin'. If ye will, I'll give ye as much apple-jack as ye kin tote away, an' keep on yer hosses."

"Let me advise you, Mrs. Hawkins," said the sergeant, "not to rebuild the house while we are here. The colonel will surely order it burned."

"We shall rebuild it," she answered, "unless Colonel Keith sets a guard over the grounds."

"He probably will not do that, madam. He will allow it to be rebuilt, just for the pleasure of burning it down."

"Is it proper for me to ask you how long he intends to remain in this neighborhood?" asked Mrs. Hawkins.

"Certainly, madam," answered the sergeant, "but I cannot tell you; though I have heard him say that he in-·
tends to stay till he has captured and hung Reuben Ellis."

The Confederates having gone, and the children being sent away, Mrs. Hawkins said to Sukey, "If you will stay here, dear, I will ride up and see Squire Plotts on the mountain."

"Ye'd better let me gwo, ma'am," said Sukey, "fur

ye'll hev ter ride all th' way round by th' woods, ter git shut uv Cunnel Keith's regiment."

"I know the way," answered Mrs. Hawkins, "and it is better for me to go; for the Squire was my husband's friend, and he may do for me what he wouldn't do for you, Sukey."

As she was slowly climbing the mountain on the back of Sam, she was halted by a sentinel, while still half a mile from the camp of the refugees. He was a man from Haywood county, and unacquainted with Mrs. Hawkins, but, on hearing her name, he allowed her to pass on to the next picket, who, he said, was one of her own neighbors. This man left his post to guide her past the other sentries whom she would meet before reaching the encampment. Evidently, Squire Plotts knew of the proximity of Keith's forces, and did not intend to be come upon without warning.

She found the Squire, reclining at his ease in Reuben Ellis's half-faced cabin, his feet encased in slippers, and his long white hair hanging loosely around his shoulders. Helping her to alight, he conducted her to one of the rustic seats, with many expressions of pleasure at having made her personal acquaintance. As soon as his complimentary volubility would permit, she said to him, "I have just learned from the men who have burned my house, that Colonel Keith intends to stay here till he has captured Reuben Ellis. No doubt he has stationed soldiers on every path by which Reuben can get here. He doesn't know that Keith has returned, and so will not be on his guard. Can't you in some way give him warning?"

"I can't see how we kin, Mrs. Hawkins," answered the Squire, "for nary a one of us knows th' route he'll come by. But do ye say th' scoundrils hev burned th' house over yer head?"

"Yes, Squire," she answered, "but let me tell you about that by and by. Now, I am anxious about Reuben. There is not a moment to lose; for, if word is not sent to him at once, he may be captured. The man who brought us Reuben's letter — he knows the route — can't he go?"

"He mout, ma'am," said the Squire, "but he's twenty mile away, ter his home in Yancey."

"No doubt some man here knows where he lives — won't you let some one go for him?"

"Certainly I will, ma'am," said the Squire, "and now that I think uv it, we've got hyar nigh onter forty uv yer naabors — lyin'-outers as hev come inter camp, thinkin' we was gwine ter hev a brush with the Rebels. It mout be as some uv them has been over the route with Reuben."

Going then to the entrance of the cabin, he put his hand to his mouth, and uttered the loud bleat of a deer, when instantly, from the near-by forest, the overhanging rocks, and the half-faced cabins in the vicinity, emerged not less than eighty stalwart mountaineers, each one armed with a rifle. They gathered quickly about the Squire, and he said to them, "If any one among ye knows th' route Reuben Ellis tucks in gwine ter Tennessee, let him come forward." Two Madison county men stepped from the ranks, and then the Squire continued, "If any one uv ye knows whar Jared Bolton's house ar', over ter Yancey, let him come forward." Another Madison county man came forward, and then the Squire went on to tell them of the danger of Ellis, and the necessity of giving him warning, ending his remarks with, "Ye'll tuck yer lives in yer hands, fur thar haint a doubt th' scoundril Keith has set his traps all through th' mountings; but I knows every man uv ye all wud be proud ter die fur Reuben Ellis."

As the three men left to make preparations for the perilous tramp through Keith's lines, the Squire turned to the others, saying, " Thar's not a doubt Keith knows whar we ar' camped, and means ter attack us. He's only waitin' fur Ellis ter come in, fur if he misses him on th' route, he counts on kotchin' him hyar; so I think ye Madison men hed best warn th' other outliers ter come ter camp to once. We shall need every man we kin git; but with all uv ye hyar, we'll lead Keith such a dance as he never tuck afore. Now, ye'll oblige me if ye'll call in th' outliers, and th' rest uv ye keep within hearin'."

As the men dispersed, the Squire, calling the attention of Mrs. Hawkins to the ledge of rocks at the rear of the camp, said, "Madam, ye see that four-foot wall I've built along the edge uv th' presurpiss. I larned in Mexico allers to fortify if thar was a rock or a sod handy. Ahind uv thet wall our men'll be bomb-proof, and kin pick off th' Rebels at their leisure."

The Squire then asked Mrs. Hawkins about the burning of her house, and she related the circumstances, adding that the men who had come on from Haywood county had better not be sent through to Tennessee, inasmuch as Ellis had decided to gather a force to drive the Confeder-

25

ates from the mountains. To this the Squire cordially assented, and he further volunteered to at once rebuild Mrs. Hawkins's dwelling. This done, he would place a guard in ambush over it, and give Keith a warm reception should he again attempt its destruction.

The route through the woods on the flank of Keith's position being unknown to the men from Haywood county, it was necessary that Mrs. Hawkins should guide their way, and accordingly a party of about twenty accompanied her on her return to her dwelling. They halted in the forest about a fourth of a mile in the rear of the burned house, until she sent to them saws and other necessary implements, and then they set to work getting out the timber and flooring for the new dwelling. Felling the trees with saws, they made not enough noise to attract attention, and had finished the work by midnight. Then, after removing the ruins of the burned dwelling they went back to their camp to return on the succeeding night and erect the house on its previous foundation.

This was done on the following night by a stronger force, under the personal superintendence of Squire Plotts, he being present mainly to direct the fight in case the work should be interrupted. There was, however, no interruption, though about midnight a mounted Confederate was seen to pass along the highway within gunshot of the dwelling. It was a moonlit night, and being able to work nearly as well as by day, the men — expert at such employment — had the house raised, the roof on, the floors laid, and the doors and windows hung by an hour before daybreak.

Then the Squire said to Mrs. Hawkins, "Thet feller ridin' along th' road shows thet Keith ar' spyin' on us. He means to attack ye during th' day or night. My advice ter ye would be ter move yer things inter th' house, but ter leave yer bed in th' barn, so ye'll be out uv th' way uv th' bullets. I'll post what men ar' hyar, jist in th' edge uv th' timber, and if ye'll lend me a horse, I'll ride stret back ter camp, and bring as many more as can be speered. By this time I reckon th' most of the outliers will have come in."

On his return to the encampment the Squire found that, with the newly-arrived reinforcements, he had a force of nearly one hundred and twenty men, all of them stalwart mountaineers, handy with the rifle, and eager to wreak vengeance upon the miscreant Keith, and his band of marauders. Leaving twenty of these men in the camp, under command of a trusty neighbor, with strict injunctions to keep sentries out in all directions, day and night, and to retire to the rocky ledge on the first approach of an enemy, he led the remainder, with all possible speed, to join their comrades in the woods in the rear of the endangered dwelling.

It was afternoon when he arrived, and from his position he could see that the house had not yet been disturbed, but he soon had direct tidings to that effect from Sukey. She brought to him the three Henry carbines which had belonged to the sons of Mrs. Hawkins. She said to him, "We hev hed these guns hid away in th' loft uv th' barn. They was th' boys, an' thar mother an' me think 'taint no more nor right tho guns should hev a chance ter tuck vengeance on th' boys' murderers. Ary one uv 'em will do as much work as sixteen common rifles."

The Squire regarded the carbines as equal to a reinforcement of fifty men, still, he hoped the attack would be deferred until after dark, for then he could place his men in ambush, in the line of shrubbery that grew directly in the rear of the original dwelling, and probably beat off the assault with little, if any, loss to his own force. In this he was not to be disappointed, for the day wore slowly away with no appearance of the Confederates, and soon after dark he moved silently forward to the position from which he expected to take them at a disadvantage.

The sky was cloudless, the moon was at the full and, shining down through the rare atmosphere of this mountain region, it shed over field and forest a light as clear, and almost as brilliant, as that of day. A dead silence brooded over every thing, broken only now and then by the hoot of an owl, or the distant howl of some wolf far away upon the mountains. Mrs. Hawkins sat with Sukey by a window of the new dwelling, in which they had made their beds, leaving Martha, the servant, to a safer lodging in the barn with the animals. Hour after hour they sat there till the brass clock upon the rude mantelpiece told that it was midnight. Then suddenly Mrs. Hawkins exclaimed, "Hark! Sukey, do you hear that?" It was a low, measured sound, coming steadily near—the distant tread of a body of horsemen.

"They are coming," she said, "coming to their death! God pity them." Then in a few moments she added, "Sukey, dear, won't you go out at the back door, and see that the men are ready." As Sukey left the room Mrs. Hawkins sank to her knees, and bowing her head upon her hands, she said, "Oh! Heavenly Father, forgive me if there is wrong in what is to happen — forgive the murderers of my poor boys; some of whom are so soon to meet human justice — and oh! forgive me, if in my heart there has been one feeling of revenge for the wrongs they have done me."

As she rose from her knees, Sukey returned to the room, saying, "They is all ready, ma'am; an' th' Squar thinks ye had best order 'em from th' yard, an' then if they doesn't go, he'll fire on 'em."

"That I will do," said Mrs. Hawkins, "and Sukey, you had better go to the barn. There is no filling between the logs — and some of the bullets may hit you."

"I'm not afeard, ma'am; an' I can't gwo ef you stay."

It was not many more minutes before a body of horsemen filed in at the gateway. They had dismounted, and were about fastening their horses to the line of fence that bordered the high-road, when, opening the door whence she could be distinctly heard, Mrs. Hawkins called to them: "Leave my grounds, you gray-coated ruffians! If you don't, your blood will be on your own heads."

A chorus of jeers and yells was the only answer to this warning. When they had died away, there came a discharge of rifle-shots from the line of shrubbery, and many a man and horse fell to the ground, never to rise again. A long-continued roll of fire followed, as if an entire regiment were in the ambuscade, and panic-stricken, the Confederates fled, leaving twenty dead and dying upon the ground behind them. A half-dozen of the horses were killed, and upwards of a score broke away, and fled up the mountain to be subsequently captured by the mountaineers. The Confederates evidently expected resistance, for the party numbered at least two hundred; but disconcerted by the sudden and long-continued volleys from their concealed enemies, they fled without firing a shot.

When Mrs. Hawkins related to me these circumstances, we stood together beside a spring upon the lower part of her lawn, near the highway, and pointing to the outlet of the spring, she said, "That run was a sight all the next day, and I've never drawn water from it since. It was a pity so many poor fellows — every one of them with a wife, a sister, or a mother — should die for one lone woman like me; but I couldn't help it. They brought it on themselves."

When the last Confederate had fled down the high-road Mrs. Hawkins, Sukey, and Squire Plotts, descended the hill to look after the wounded. Three only were alive, among them the fair-haired young sergeant who had shown so much courtesy to Mrs. Hawkins. The three were taken tenderly up by a half-dozen of the mountaineers, and borne to the house, where they were laid upon the beds already prepared for Mrs. Hawkins and Sukey. Two died before the morning, but the young sergeant, though desperately wounded, lived through the night, and finally, after two months of most watchful attendance, was able to leave his bed, and walk about the grounds. In another month he joined Reuben Ellis's company of rangers, and he never again fought for the Confederacy.

CHAPTER XII.

A BATTLE BY MOONLIGHT.

COLONEL KEITH was not altogether lost to the common feelings of humanity. On the morning after the defeat of his men, he dispatched one of his soldiers to the dwelling of Mrs. Hawkins, with a letter to her asking permission to remove his killed and wounded, and pledging his honor that, in case his request was granted, he would make no further attempt to injure her property. With the first appearance of daylight, Squire Plotts had fallen back to the woods at the rear of the house, and he could not now be consulted without disclosing his position to the soldier; Mrs. Hawkins was, therefore, obliged to act upon her own judgment. "The men are all dead," she said to the soldier, "excepting one — Sergeant Blount — who is in the house, very badly wounded. I will take Colonel Keith's word, because, if he should now burn my house, he would inevitably kill his own officer; for any attempt to remove him will be fatal. However, he can send not more than twenty men, and the bodies must be removed to-day. If they are not away by nightfall, I shall have them buried."

This being made known to the Squire after the departure of the messenger, he set out at once for Spring Mountain, leaving, however, a dozen of his men to see, from behind the line of shrubbery, that Keith's soldiers conducted themselves in an orderly manner. During the day the dead bodies were removed, and, meanwhile, some aged men among the neighbors volunteered to chink the crevices between the logs of the dwelling, and put the grounds in order. This they did, and by nightfall no vestige of the recent carnage remained, except the bent grass, trodden by the feet of many horses, and the crimsoned rivulet below the spring, which still ran with the blood of the men whose bodies had been borne away to unknown graves among the mountains. On the following day the school resumed its sessions, and the place took on its usual tranquil appearance. One ignorant of the events, looking then upon that sloping lawn, lying there so green and wavy in the sun, would not have imagined that it had been so recently the scene whence so many hapless souls had rushed unbidden into the stern realities of the future life.

It was on the second day of the school, and shortly before noon, when Martha entered the school-room, and in a low tone announced to Mrs. Hawkins that Justin was at the front entrance, desiring to see her. Saying nothing to Sukey, she rose, and went out to meet him. As he stood by the dining-room door she was startled by his altered appearance. He was hollow-eyed, and his face was pale and haggard. His clothes sat upon him loosely, as if his robust frame had dwindled to two-thirds of its former proportions, and there was in his bloodshot eyes a look so wild, craven, and dejected, that Mrs. Hawkins regarded him with involuntary pity, despite the abundant cause she had for a severer feeling. Still, there was some sternness in her tone as she asked, "What is it that you want of me?"

"To tell ye, ma'am, that Reuben Ellis have got through safely." This he said avoiding her glance, but in a tone which showed that he was aware he was the bearer of welcome tidings.

"Thank God! thank God!" she exclaimed; but in a moment she added, "How do you know this? Have you seen him?"

"I haint seed him," he answered, "but I had hit not two hours ago from a man as had seed him He fell inter a trap ez Cunnel Keith had sot for him. Thar was a dozen agin him, and they killed his nag; but his sixteen shooter saved him. He shot three or four uv 'em, and then, got inter th' thick undergrowth whar they was afeard ter foller. Hit war about midnight, and he must hev fotched th' camp on Spring Mountain afore this time."

"It is good news, Robert Justin," rejoined Mrs. Hawkins. "I was very anxious about him, and I greatly thank you for bringing me this word. If this is all you have to say, I will now go back to the school."

"I has more, ma'am," he said, "uv life and death importance ter ye and Reuben; but I daren't say it hyar — hit would cost me my life ef hit was know'd I hed betrayed 'em. Ef ye'll let me step inter th' house, I'll tell ye."

"Very well, come in," she said, leading him into the dining-room, and pointing to a chair. "I'll be glad to hear you; but please be brief, for I must go back to the school presently." "Hit ar' this, ma'am, Cunnel Keith

26

have comed hyar, and stayed hyar, only ter druv ye away, and tuck and hang Reube Ellis. He thinks hit's all along uv ye two thet he's got no recruits in th' mountings. When he yered Reube was away, he sot traps fur him nigh all th' way ter Tennessee; but, being ez he had a horse, Reuben must hev come th' travilled roads, and so escaped 'em. Now, thet th' Cunnel knows he have got through, he swars he'll hev him, or die in tryin'. He means ter attack th' camp on Spring Mountain ter night. He knows all about hit — thet Squire Plotts have got only seventy men — and he's got more'n five hundred, some uv 'em with Winchester rifles.''

Mrs. Hawkins had remarkable control over her features, or Justin might have seen that she believed his report, and felt a sudden fear for the safety of the mountaineers: however, despite her alarm, she asked coolly, "How does Colonel Keith know all about the camp?"

"From a Shelton Laurel man, as he has tuck, and given his life fur tellin' him."

"And how do you know that he intends to attack the camp to-night?" she asked, looking him intently in the face.

"'Case he telled me so," he answered, "not more'n two hours ago."

"I believe you," she said, her manner softening toward him, "and though you are betraying your friends, I thank you. You are making some amends for the great wrong you have done me."

"I never meant ter do ye wrong, ma am," he said, his face lighting up with something like a hopeful expression.

"I would do ary thing ter serve ye; and now ez I has showed ye thet I would, will ye let me ax ye ter do suthin' fur me?"

"What is it?" asked Mrs. Hawkins.

"Ter speak a kind word fur me ter Sukey. I can't live without her, ma'am. Ye sees what I ar'—the shadder uv what I was—hit's all along uv Sukey—I must hev her again ter live with, and love me—and she kin love me, ma'am, fur I haint th' man I was—I'se repented in dust and ashes."

She involuntarily moved her seat farther from him, and a look of inexpressible loathing came upon her features, as she said, "So, it is for this you have given me this warning—to make me your tool to seduce a pure soul again into your slimy clutches. Robert Justin, there is a God, and the one thing He absolutely hates is falsehood, and you are steeped in it to the very core. For a filthy reward you betrayed my poor boys, and now, to serve your vile passions, you have been false to their murderers. In revealing what you have, God has made you His instrument for saving a true and loyal man, and inflicting a deeper punishment upon yourself—for you have placed an impassable gulf between yourself and Sukey. When I tell her of this, she will loathe you more than I do." Then rising from her chair, with an imperious tone and manner, she added, "Now go, and never cross my path again."

With a bowed head, and a craven look, Justin staggered out from the door-way. When he had gone, Mrs. Hawkins went to the school-room, and said to Sukey,

"Have one of the older boys put saddle and bridle upon Sam, immediately. Then come to my room for a moment." As she was changing her garments for the trip to the camp on the mountain, she related to Sukey her interview with Justin. · When she had finished the narration, Sukey said, "Why he ar' worse nor Judas; and I've know'd hit, ma'am, ever sence I woke up ter know right from wrong."

At the camp the situation was discussed between Squire Plotts and Reuben Ellis in the presence of Mrs. Hawkins. Both were in favor of standing their ground, and risking an engagement. They would be greatly outnumbered, but the camp could be approached only in front; and from behind their stone-wall barricade, they could pick off one-half of their assailants, before the other half should have reached the foot of the rocky ledge on which they would be posted. A victory was, therefore, reasonably certain, and it would doubtless drive Keith from the district. Moreover, such an one, gained at that time, before the officer detailed by General Burnside had arrived, would give the mountaineers confidence in themselves, and greatly contribute toward freeing the mountain region from the presence of the Confederates. These considerations decided them to risk a battle, and Mrs. Hawkins went to her home well knowing that another scene of blood and horror was to be enacted before another morning.

"Oh! Sukey," she said, putting her arms about her, when she had told her of this resolve of the leaders, "I wish we were in some other world, where there is not all this strife and violence."

"I don't know, ma'am," replied Sukey, "haint it so everywhar — the evil allers strugglin' agin th' good? In the Bible ye guv me, hit says thar was war in heaven. But Michael cast out th' dragon; and musn't it allers be so, seein' th' Lord ar' on th' side uv th' right, and won't see hit finarly gwo under? Th' odds ar' great agin 'em; but th' Bible hit say th' battle ar' not ter th' strong; but th' Lord of Hosts, he giveth th' victory. So, I shill pray ter Him, and He nuver yit has refused my prayer — never sence I made up my full mind ter be one uv His children."

Again it was a clear, moonlit night, and silence reigned over all the mighty forest. Except the occasional cry of some wild creature, not a sound was heard as hour after hour the men stood at their posts, listening with strained ears for the distant tread of their assailants. All were well armed — Ellis, the Squire, and two expert marksmen, with carbines, the others with the long-barreled mountain rifle — and the two flanks of their position, approachable only on the hands and knees, had been further strengthened by a high barricade of logs. No sentinels were out, for sentries were useless so long as an attack was certain. Every man was in his assigned place, and each one had heard the words of Ellis, "Single out your man — don't fire till sure of your aim — and remember that these are the men who have killed the Hawkins boys, burned your homes, and murdered your dearest kindred."

Not far from midnight a distant rustling roar like the

steady sweep of an autumn wind, was heard coming up from the lower part of the mountain. Gradually it came nearer till it could be distinguished that two columns were advancing, one against each flank of the entrenchment. " They will be upon us soon," now cried Ellis. " Every man to his knees, and except when he fires, keep his head below the line of the wall. Don't shoot till I give the word ; then load and fire as fast as you can, and we'll score off the debt we owe these devils."

Thus they waited for perhaps a quarter of an hour, till Keith's men emerged from among the trees, and began to form in two solid bodies, about twenty-five front, by ten deep, at the edge of the open space on which stood the encampment. The evident intention was to simultaneously storm the two flanks of the barricade, and carry them by mere weight of numbers. They were now not much more than two hundred yards away, but Ellis waited till the two masses were well compacted — broad targets for his unerring mountain rifles. Then the word " Fire " rang along the cliff, and two sheets of shotted flame poured down upon the assailants. For ten long minutes the fiery death continued to fall, till not a Confederate was to be seen except those who were on the ground either killed or wounded. They fired but one round, and that drew blood from only two of the mountaineers. Keith himself is said to have been far in the rear ; but had he been at the front, and a braver man than he was, he could not have held his men to their posts an instant longer. Human nature at its best estate, is not a stable mark for more than a hundred mountain rifles.

On the following day Keith abandoned the district, leaving his dead and wounded to the mercy of the men he had driven from their homes, and whose nearest kindred he had mercilessly slaughtered. A reckoning had not yet come for him, for "the mills of the gods grind slowly."

CHAPTER XIII.

SOME EXPLOITS OF COLONEL GEORGE W. KIRK.

COLONEL GEORGE W. KIRK, the officer who was detailed by General Burnside to organize the loyal mountaineers, is a man not highly esteemed by the late disloyal element of the North Carolina Alleghanies. Among more than a score of intelligent and upright residents of that region whom I conversed with, I failed to hear one allude to him except in terms of the strongest reprobation. But this may merely illustrate the fact that our opinions depend very much upon the point from which we view things, and are often warped by our individual interests and convictions.

I have no personal knowledge of Colonel Kirk; have never so much as communicated with him; but from an unbiased investigation, aimed solely at the truth, I have been led to the conclusion that he was brave, enterprising, and humane, and also endowed with very many of the qualities that gave Sumpter and Marion so honorable a place in Southern history. His skill as a military man was remarkable, his vigilance never slept, his activity was untiring, and some of his exploits exhibit a dashing boldness that recalls the days of knight-errantry, and would have won him a brilliant reputation had he enjoyed a wider field of operations. Moreover, the mountaineers whom he commanded, had for him, and still have, an enthusiastic admiration, which of itself implies that he possessed more than ordinary skill, bravery, and humanity. I have been obliged to form a very favorable estimate of his character, but the facts I relate concerning him, are derived from his enemies, as well as his friends.

With only a handful of men Colonel Kirk entered Madison county, but so rapidly did the mountain men flock to his quarters that in a few days his force numbered four hundred, whom he at once proceeded to drill in the tactics of regular warfare. The whereabouts of Keith were not known; but it was supposed that he had joined Bragg at Chickamauga, and it was hoped that his recent defeat, and the presence of so considerable a body of Union troops, would deter any formidable number of Confederates from again intruding upon the district. In these circumstances, it not being in his nature to remain inactive, Kirk proposed to his men an expedition into East Tennessee, where Longstreet was besieging Knoxville, and the disloyal element along the western base of the mountains, inspirited by the result of the recent battle of Chickamauga, was giving much trouble to the Union inhabitants. The major part of his force was composed of "outliers"— men who had resorted to the woods rather than absent themselves from the vicinity of their wives and children — but they did not now hesitate to leave their homes, which is evidence of the ascendency that Kirk had already — in less than two months — acquired over them. It was now November, and the mountain men remained in Tennessee until the following

27

July, but their operations there do not fall within the scope of my narrative.

Meanwhile, not a solitary Confederate soldier disturbed the quiet of Madison county. Even Parson Justin had relieved the district of his abhorred presence — abhorred now that his dishonesty and treachery had become generally known in the community. From the day that, baffled and crestfallen, he had slunk away from Mrs. Hawkins's door, he was never again seen in that neighborhood. Her scathing words had shown him the utter hopelessness of any further pursuit of Sukey, and, realizing this, he probably began to reckon up the gains of his wickedness. What had it profited him — the pilfering from his distressed neighbors, the betrayal of the wretch Keith, who had trusted him, and the incited murder of the sons of his benefactress? Then, possibly, the light broke in upon him, and he saw himself in his naked vileness; and, unable to endure the sight, he fled away to where he would not be continually reminded of his crimes. However, if he felt remorse, it did not lead him to repentance, for it was not long before he resumed his career of fraud and treachery, though his crimes were never again attended with such bloody consequences.

But the district had not yet taken final leave of the butcher Keith, and his myrmidons. He passed through it in July, 1864, on his way to the vicinity of Morganton, in Burke county. He tarried but a single day, but in that one day he left a trail of blood behind him. He captured five men near the Shelton Laurel, and with no reasonable motive — in, apparently, pure wantonness —

"murdered all of them," says Daniel Ellis, "in a most shocking and barbarous manner."

When this atrocity became known to Mrs. Hawkins, she saw that the neighborhood could have no permanent peace and security without the constant presence in it of a strong body of loyal soldiery; and instantly she decided to set out to find Colonel Kirk, and induce him to return to Tennessee. She did not know where he was, nor what obstacles and dangers she might have to encounter in reaching him; but these considerations did not deter her, and without delay she set out alone and unattended. In her saddle-bags she put a few days' rations, and in a sack behind her, a couple of bushels of corn for Sam to nibble upon in the failure of other provender; and thus equipped, she plunged into a region supposed to be infested with bushwhackers, and other disorderly characters, among whom an unprotected woman had about the same chance for safety as a solitary lamb among a pack of wolves.

She did not even know the roads which she would have to travel, never having been that way before; but taking the bridle-path down the Laurel river, she was soon at the French Broad, along which then ran a good highway to the Warm Springs. Here she found the immense caravansary, which for many years has been a noted summer resort, hermetically closed, and the mansion of its proprietor — seated on a gentle hill at a little distance — equally deserted. As she approached the latter, however, she caught sight of an antiquated negro — too old to run away, and not valuable enough to be stolen — lolling under the shade of a tree near the dwelling. "Good morning, Uncle," she said to him. "Mornin', Missy," he answered, raising himself, half-awake, upon his elbow.

"Are you the only one in the neighborhood, Uncle?" she inquired.

"Nary anudder soul yere 'cept ole Pomp, Missy. Jess now he'm de sole 'prietor ob all dese housin an' lands," he answered. "You sees, Missy, it wasn't bery healfy yere fur massa when Cunnel Kirk comed round, so he tuck a streak o' lightnin' inter de 'Federacy, and leff ebery ting ter old Pomp. Dat was what Pomp telled de Cunnel, when he stayed yere ober night wid him sogers — dat de hull place b'long ter Pomp, an' he was Union clar fru ter de back-bone."

"And what did the colonel say to that?" asked Mrs. Hawkins, smiling.

"Why he jess laff, an' he say widout a doubt it orter be so, 'case Pomp had a wuck'd fur it all him life. An' den he ax ef massa was a good massa, an' Pomp telled him dar wasn't never anudder so good sence de Lord called ole Abram — him as we hab now fur President — an' dat am de Lord's trufh, Missy, 'case Pomp brung him up his own self."

"Then you are Union, and your master is Secesh," said Mrs. Hawkins, laughing. "That's a convenient arrangement."

"Dat'm jess 'cordin' ter circumstances, Missy. Massa say Pomp am like de great 'postle — all tings ter all men — Union wid de Union, Secesh wid de Secesh. It doan't make nary difference ter him, so long as he an' massa gits off wid a hull skin. An' Pomp counts on doin' dat 'case Cunnel Kirk am a gemman — a clar gemman, Missy."

"And where is Colonel Kirk now, Uncle?"

"Doan't egzactly know, Missy — sum whar up ter Tennessee. Pomp haint seed him fur a long, long while. But you needn't be afeard ter travil dat way, fur de Cunnel hab cleaned out all de Secesh, an' de bushwhackers. Dey darn't come widin forty mile ob him ; fur dey say he rides like de whirlygust, an' fights like de bery ole debil."

"Well, good-bye, Uncle," said Mrs. Hawkins, preparing to ride away. "But tell me, Uncle — where can I get dinner ?"

"Ter Squar Ottinger's, 'bout two mile up de road — de brick house, de only one any whar 'bout. You'll hab a good dinner dar ; but 'cuse me, Missy — you'd better not leff dem know who you am, nor whar you'se gwine, fur de Squar an' him wife am most ez much like de ole 'postle ez Pomp am."

"Then *you* know who I am ?" said Mrs. Hawkins.

"Yas, Missy, Pomp knowd you jess so soon as he sot eyes on you' hoss, fur dat nag was along when you' brave boys was yere arter gittin' Reuben Ellis frum under de gallus. An' Pomp know whar you'm gwine, fur two ob de Shelton men ez hed got off frum de killin', staid yere ober night only yesterday. Dey was gwine on ter Cunnel Kirk, like you am ; an' Pomp hope you'll find him, an' brung him back ter rid de yearth ob dat ole debil, Keith."

"So, you are a good Union man, after all," said Mrs. Hawkins, laughing.

"Dat depends on who Pomp's a talkin' ter, Missy," answered the negro, grinning; "but he gwo fur you, an' fur eberybody ez sarves de good Lord like you do. An' so he make bold ter say, Missy, dat you'd better not stop ter Ottinger's, but ride stret on ter Squar Allen's, ter Wolf creek. You kin git dar afore sundown. De Squar am a good, true man, an' so am him sister, what keep house fur him. Dey'll keep you ober night like a lady, an' it'm likely de Squar kin tole you whar Cunnel Kirk am; fur he'm a Union man, an' he hain't afeard to say so."

Thanking the old negro warmly for this timely advice, Mrs. Hawkins rode on up the high-road, and about an hour before sunset, alighted at the door-way of Squire Allen's dwelling. Every traveler in that part of the world knows that quaint, old-fashioned mansion, nestling among the hills, its low roof and broad veranda, over-hung with wide-branching trees that have given a grate-ful shelter to numberless weary strangers for more than half a century. Very pleasant is it to the tired wayfarer to come upon it when all the outer world is sweltering in the July heat, and to have the breeze which comes down the mountain gorge, fan his cheek with the cool breath of October; but heated, dusty, and weary as she was, more grateful to Mrs. Hawkins than that shady porch, or that refreshing breeze, was the greeting she received from the kindly host and hostess of the mansion. No sooner did she mention her name than they gave her much such a welcome as, I suppose, awaits all good men and women on their first entrance into the better country.

Here she rested for the night, and soon after daybreak on the following morning set out again on her journey, satisfied from the information her host had given her, that she would come up with Reuben Ellis and Colonel Kirk by nightfall.   In this she was not disappointed. She found them encamped on the French Broad, in Tennessee, about a mile north of Newport.   The men from Shelton Laurel were there before her, so it was not necessary to tell her errand.   Colonel Kirk had already decided to return into North Carolina, and his men were in readiness to set out on the march on the following morning. "But," he said to Mrs. Hawkins, "it is not enough to station a force in Madison county.   We must end that man's career, and that Ellis and I, and these brave boys, will do within a fortnight."

At sunset on the second day following, Kirk and his command went into camp on the open ground in the rear of Mrs. Hawkins's dwelling, and that very night Reuben Ellis, disguised, and mounted on the back of Sam, set out on a trip below the Blue Ridge, to ascertain the whereabouts of Keith and his forces.   On foot, and along secluded by-paths the journey would have been extremely perilous, for it was venturing into the very heart of the Confederacy; but on horseback, and along traveled roads, it seemed to Colonel Kirk nothing short of foolhardy. "It won't do," he said to Ellis, "you won't be gone a day before they have you."   "I wouldn't venture it," answered Ellis, " with any other horse in the known world; but this pony will keep silent, and do just as I tell him.

Besides, I shall travel only at night, and I know every foot of the way, if, as the word goes, he is near Morganton."

"Well," said Kirk, "the chances are if we don't strike him soon, he'll join some larger body, and so escape us. But the danger is great, and I wouldn't like to lose you, Ellis."

"Never fear," replied Reuben, "we'll be back within a week — I and the pony," and with these words he rode off into the darkness.

A week passed and nothing was seen or heard of Ellis, and then three more days went away without tidings of him, and Mrs. Hawkins and Colonel Kirk were about giving him up for lost, when just at dark one cloudy day, the sentry down the road was heard to give a succession of loud shouts, and in a moment more Ellis rode up to the door-way of Mrs. Hawkins. She had heard the shouts, and hastened to the door, and then, as he sprang from the back of Sam, she threw her arms about him, and with glad tears, cried "Oh! my boy, my dear Reuben! What should I have done if they had taken *you?*"

There was joy that night in that household, in that camp, and among those mountains wherever the news had spread, over the marvelous escape of Reuben Ellis.

For two days and nights he had lain concealed in a clump of laurels, while the Confederates, having surrounded the woods, were beating its every bush, and exploring its every little cluster of timber. One moonlight night he had fallen among a party of twenty, well mounted. Three of their bullets went through his hat, one cut off a lock of hair just above his ear, and another grazed the flank of Sam ; but, thanks to the pony's heels, he got away uninjured. A still narrower escape he had at the base of Table Rock Mountain. All of fifty surrounded him there, and he got away only by leaping from a high bank into the Linville river, and then by fording, and swimming several miles down the stream — going back on his route —until he struck a wooded ravine. There he lay for two days and one night, hearing the baying of the hounds all around him. Had he not balked their scent by taking to the water, his career would, then and there, have ended.

These were some of the incidents of the perilous trip, and at first sight it may well be accounted foolhardy. It is its result that lifts it into the heroic, for Ellis had looked down on Keith's encampment, and counted the men that were with him. They numbered seven hundred —Keith's own command, and that of some superior officer. But they were without intrenchments, and resting in absolute security, knowing nothing of any Union force nearer than Tennessee, a hundred and fifty miles distant.

That night in the sitting-room of Mrs. Hawkins Colonel Kirk and Reuben Ellis discussed the situation. The country through which the Union troops would have to pass thronged with Confederates. Seven hundred were near Morganton, fifteen hundred or two thousand were at Asheville, and smaller bands were scattered everywhere throughout the region east of Buncombe county. Kirk had only three hundred and twenty-five men, and by the circuitous route he would have to travel to flank

28

the force at Asheville, he would traverse nearly two hundred miles of hostile country, where intelligence of his every movement would be quickly communicated to his armed enemies. Thus, if he should reach unmolested his objective point, and succeed in defeating more than twice his own number, he would still have the Asheville garrison in his rear, and doubtless be speedily surrounded by several thousand enemies. It would be a desperate enterprise. The Confederates speak of it as foolhardy; but a more appropriate term is heroic; for every step was carefully calculated, every contingency clearly foreseen and provided for. Kirk well understood the terrible odds against him, but he thoroughly knew his soldiers. They had been long enough together to become merged into one individuality, of which he was the brain, they the body; and he counted on his own skill, and on the eager desire of his men to wreak vengeance upon Keith and his myrmidons.

So, on the following morning, with his three hundred and twenty-five men, he set out on the hazardous expedition. Striking due east into Yancey county, he crossed Mitchell county a few miles south of Bakersville, and, a little before noon of the second day's ride, forded the North Fork of the Catawba river. Here he fell in with an old hunter who, suspecting his errand, volunteered to guide him by an unfrequented, but direct route, to a wooded hill in the rear of Keith's encampment. Two hours before sunset the troop crossed Linville river, at the point where Ellis came near to falling into the hands of the Confederates; and in another hour they stood upon the slope of Table Rock, and looked down through the clear air upon the steeples of Morganton.

Morganton was then, and is now, a thriving town of a thousand people, and the centre of a wide agricultural region. A country road leads directly to it, but if Kirk followed it, the danger was that his men might chance upon some one who would hasten before them to Keith, and apprise him of their coming. Therefore, they climbed another half mile up the mountain, and waited there for darkness to come on, when, guided by the old hunter, they could hope to escape all notice from the inhabitants.

Had they been in the mood to enjoy the picturesque in nature, their eyes might have feasted, while they were waiting there for the sun to go down, upon a view beyond all comparison more wild and sublime than any to be seen in North Carolina. But I doubt if they were in such a mood, for darkness no sooner fell than they set out again on their march. Scarcely more than fifteen miles now separated them from the Confederate encampment, and they moved forward slowly and cautiously, Kirk riding by the side of the guide, and Ellis directly in his rear, each with his pistol ready to pronounce his doom at the first evidence his actions should give of treachery.

But, no treachery was intended or attempted, and just at midnight they fell upon the sleeping Confederates, and killed or captured the entire number, together with all their stores and animals. Not a man or an officer escaped. So clean a sweep, effected by a greatly inferior force, in the heart of the enemy's country, did not, so far as I know, occur in any of the minor operations of the civil war.

Colonel Kirk had now before him the most difficult and
dangerous part of his adventurous expedition.   How was
he to break through the cordon of Confederate forces,
which, within thirty-six hours, would be drawn closely
around him?   But both attack and escape had been carefully planned in the sitting-room of Mrs. Hawkins, and,
I am told, that all resulted precisely as he had foreseen,
except that he was disappointed in the large number of
prisoners captured.   He had planned not to return by
the way he came, for he counted that intelligence of his
forward march would be at once sent to Asheville, and
that doubtless, his object would be guessed, and a strong
force be moving upon his rear before he should arrive at
Morganton.   But, he was informed, that south of the
Swannanoa there was no considerable body of Confederates, and that a good road led through Hickory Nut Gap
to the upper French Broad, and thence on to Waynesville.
This road he intended to take, and thus flank Asheville
on the south, while the troops from that place should be
looking for him in the vicinity of Morganton.   Once at
Waynesville ten hours in advance of pursuit, he would be
in safety, for a ride of thirty hours along the Big Pigeon
would bring him to General Gillam, at Knoxville.

What embarrassed Kirk was that which he had not foreseen —his large number of prisoners.   His coming upon
the Confederates had been a complete surprise, and half-
awake, and cut off from their arms, they had been able to
inflict no damage upon their captors.   Therefore, every
mountaineer was fit for duty, but each man had to guard
two others, while galloping at the rapid rate of six or eight

miles an hour. But thus they marched — each Union trooper between two Confederates—the latter riding their own horses, and bearing their own unloaded muskets—and in less than three days, they arrived, not a man missing, at Knoxville. Colonel Keith had been, all the way, under the special guard of Reuben Ellis. Only this had saved his life, for many of the men had sworn to execute summary vengeance upon him before they should reach Tennessee. The prisoners were speedily transferred to Johnson's Island, and there Keith had leisure to reflect upon his crimes until the war was over.

In its boldness, celerity, and astonishing success, this raid of Colonel Kirk's bears a striking resemblance to the famous expedition of King's Mountain; and, what is very remarkable, a majority of the men in Kirk's command were direct descendants of the heroes, who, in that famous battle, turned the tide of the Revolution.

Within a fortnight from his setting out on this expedition, Colonel Kirk was back at his previous encampment near Newport; but he soon removed his quarters to Warm Springs, in order to be within striking distance of both Madison county, and the region along the foot of the mountains. As he had anticipated, when his advance into North Carolina became known at Asheville, the officer in command there sent out a strong force to intercept his return from Morganton. This force going east passed him on the flank, as he was marching westward through Hickory Nut Gap, and not more than ten miles from Asheville. Great was the universal chagrin when it was known that he had escaped with so large a body of prisoners; and no sooner was it noised abroad that he had taken up his quarters at Warm Springs, than the Confederates resolved to equip a force for his capture or destruction.

Colonel Kirk was known to have not more than three hundred and fifty men, quartered in the hotel at the Springs, with no other defenses than such as could be formed by barricading the doors and windows. A force twice as large as his own ought, certainly, to effect his capture, if it should come upon him unawares and completely surround his position. This being clear to the Confederates, a body of eight hundred picked men, well-armed and well-mounted, set out about noon one day for Warm Springs, by the road along the French Broad river. They arrived at Marshall about an hour before sunset, and there halted to refresh themselves and their animals.

While the troop was waiting there they were seen by a little woman, in modest attire, who happened to look out from the door-way of a log-house on the brow of the mountain, about a mile and a half away, as the bird flies. She gazed at them long and earnestly. What could have brought that number of gray-coated soldiers to Marshall? She sat down upon a bench before the house, a little boy beside her, to watch their movements. Soon she observed them divide into two bodies of about equal numbers, and set forward down the river. On arriving at the blacksmith's shop, she saw the forward body turn to the right up the road that climbs the Walnut Mountains, while the other kept directly on by the highway along the river.

Instantly the truth flashed upon her. The Confederates were marching to attack Colonel Kirk, and they had separated into two bodies in order to completely surround him. If they did not halt by the way they would be upon him by midnight, and taken by surprise, and by so large a force, his chance would be desperate. He must be warned; but who could be found to tell him of his danger. There was not a man within a mile, and time was precious. She must herself go, and go through the woods — fifteen miles and more — for the soldiers were on the only two roads that led to Kirk's head-quarters. This resolution taken, she led the little boy into the house, told him his mother might be away all night, but he must be a little man, and take good care of his little brother; and then, putting her sun-bonnet upon her head, and locking the cottage door, she set out along the brow of the mountain to follow the soldiers who had taken the route along the river. The little boy was Robby — now about eight years old — the little woman was Phebe Ellis.

The soldiers were evidently in no haste to reach their destination, for they traveled at so slow a pace that Phebe had no difficulty in keeping up with them. Now and then they were hidden by some overhanging cliff, or abrupt bend of the road and river; but she kept them nearly continuously in sight until they arrived at Stack-house's, a summer resort perched upon a high bluff, less than five miles from Warm Springs. Here the road is shut in by the river on one side, and steep cliffs on the other, with not much more of level space than will allow a couple of vehicles to pass abreast; but in this narrow space Phebe saw the troop halt, and prepare to go into bivouac along the highway. The sight relieved her mind greatly, for it assured her that it might be several hours before they moved forward upon Kirk's forces. She had heard that night attacks were most often made in the still hours just before morning; for then men sleep the most soundly, and this she thought to be the intention of the Confederates.

Phebe had now come nearly ten miles, the most of the distance through open woods where it was not difficult to find her way, or keep her footing, but the remainder of her route — all of five miles — would be over the rough-est and wildest portion of the Walnut Mountains, through tangled undergrowth, across rapid streams, along steep rocky ledges, and amidst a dense forest where the wolf, the catamount, and the panther, had their lairs, and roamed for their prey after nightfall. No woman had ever invaded those gloomy woods; nor even a man, except by daylight, and armed with a trusty rifle. She would have tried to descend the cliffs some distance below, and thus reach the high-road in advance of the encampment; but she had observed several mounted men go down this road, and she knew they would interrupt her progress. She had, there-fore, no alternative but to cross that dismal mountain. So, giving one prayer to God, and one glance up at the moon to judge how long she would have its light, she strode forward into the gloomy forest. How she got through I do not know, and probably she could not have told had she been questioned; but some invisible power must have guided and guarded her, for a little before midnight she emerged from the forest and approached the Union picket at the crossing of the French Broad river. He was a

Madison county man, and he knew her. "Why, Phebe!" he said, "ar' hit ye?"

"Yes," answered Phebe; "I want to see my husband."

"He hain't hyar," said the man. "He's away sence yester night—up beyant Newport, I reckon."

"Then, won't you take me ter Cunnel Kirk? I must see him directly."

"Can't leave my post, Phebe," he answered, "but ye kin gwo stret across th' bridge, an' ter them two winders whar ye see th' lights. Thet's th' Cunnel's office—ye'll find him thar. An' doan't ye be afeard; if they halt ye, just say, 'Chrismus is a comin''—that's the password for ter night."

She was stopped at the farther end of the bridge, and on two other occasions; but on each occasion she spoke the magic words, and was allowed to go forward. Then she ascended the long veranda that runs along the entire front of the huge hotel, and rapped at the door of the room whence the light proceeded. "Come in," issued from the interior, and opening the door she entered a large, well-lighted apartment. Three young men in blue uniforms were in the room, two seated upon chairs canted against the wall, the other lolling upon a sofa, in an easy attitude. The latter rose to his feet as she entered, and turned to Phebe with a look of inquiry; this look, however, soon changed to one of astonishment, as he and the others scanned her appearance. She had lost her bonnet, her hair was disheveled, brier scratches seamed her face, her dress was torn in many places, her shoes were cut through and through, and her feet, lacerated

29

by the sharp, flinty rocks, left blood-stains on the floor as she moved forward to a vacant chair, and sinking into it, said faintly, "Will you take me ter Cunnel Kirk?"

"Certainly, Madam," answered the young man, promptly opening an inner door, and exchanging a few words with some one in the adjoining room. In a moment he turned again to Phebe, saying, "Step this way, Madam. The colonel is here, and will see you."

She entered the room, took the first convenient chair, and looked at the colonel for a moment without speaking. He was seated at a desk, littered over with papers, and engaged in writing; but rising as Phebe seated herself he said, "Good evening, Madam. What can I do for you?"

"I am Reuben Ellis's wife," she answered, "and I have come near fifteen miles through the woods since dark ter warn ye that the Rebels are coming upon ye."

"What!" he exclaimed; "fifteen miles over the Walnut Mountains? Couldn't you have come by the road?"

"No, sir," she answered, "they are on both roads — the one along the French Broad, and that down the Laurel. On either of them they would have stopped me."

"Well, it's plain," he said, "that you're been through briers and underbrush."

"I have, sir," she answered, "and over a route that even a man would find it hard ter travel. Many a time I sank down tired out with falling over logs, and sharp rocks in the dark; and I never could have got through but for thinking of you as is fighting for us, and — of my husband."

"It was very brave — it was heroic, of you, Madam," he said, resuming his seat. "Please tell me all about it; where the Rebels are, and how many there are of them."

She then related to him what is already known to the reader, his keen eye meanwhile fixed intently, but kindly, upon her. He evidently believed her report, and was already revolving in his mind what measures he should take in the emergency. When she had concluded he said, "You are very tired, and I dislike to fatigue you further, but I would like to have you tell this to some of my officers. I will give you a room and a bed directly afterward where you can stay until you are thoroughly rested."

She assented, and going to the door, he spoke to one of his orderlies. Returning to his seat, he said to her, "This is very commendable in you, Mrs. Ellis. No doubt you have saved the lives of a good many of us; but you may be easy about your husband. He is safe, whatever happens. I have sent him down the river to scatter some bushwhackers. I haven't a man equal to him at that business."

In about a quarter of an hour several officers entered the room, among them, as Phebe saw by their uniforms, a major, and four captains. When she had briefly retold her story, one of the captains — a man past middle age, with a stern, hard-featured face, and a somewhat cynical expression, said to her abruptly: "How do you know there were four hundred men in each squad?"

"The men that went along the river," she answered, "rode five abreast, and I counted eighty rows of them; and I reckoned thar was as many that went up the mountain."

Then the captain plied her with a rapid succession of similar questions, till Phebe, worn out with fatigue, and dazzled by the unaccustomed sight of so much gilt lace, became confused and gave contradictory replies. Turning to Colonel Kirk, the captain then said, "She is a fraud. She contradicts herself. She is not the wife of Ellis. It is some trap the Rebels are trying to spring upon us."

The colonel smiled, and looked approvingly at Phebe, but said nothing. Seeing that he made no reply, the major spoke. "She is no fraud," he said, in a decided tone. "If you think so, look at her torn clothes, and the blood trickling from her shoes. I tell you she is honest, and more than honest — she is heroic. Not ten women in North Carolina would have done what she has done; and I think I recognize her — I think I have seen her with Reuben Ellis."

His kindly words restored Phebe to self-possession, and she said, "I have seen you, Major Rollins — before the war, ter Marshall. But Cunnel, if you doubt my being Phebe Ellis, send for Jeems Burns, the sentry ter the further side of the bridge. He knows me."

"I don't doubt you, Mrs. Ellis," said Colonel Kirk; "I haven't doubted you for a moment. The captain has no faith in man or woman; but he's a gentleman, and he'll apologize to you when we are through with this business." Then, speaking to his officers, he added, "Mrs. Ellis is right. The Rebels, four hundred strong, are at Stackhouse's; another body has come down the mountain road, and is by this time in the woods, on the rising ground in our rear. They intend to come upon us together, in front and rear, and crush us as between an upper and a nether millstone, just before daybreak. Counting out the eighty men who are away with Ellis, we haven't three hundred to meet these eight hundred. Now, what shall we do, gentlemen? Let me hear first from you, captain, and be good enough to be brief, for (drawing out his watch) it is now nearly one o'clock, and we've not more than four hours before us."

"My plan would be," said the captain, "to put the men under arms at once; post fifty at this end of the bridge, one hundred at the rear of the building, and hold the rest in readiness to defend whichever point should be first attacked. Then, at daybreak, I would send the men to bed, to sleep off the false alarm."

"Thus saith doubting Thomas," said the colonel, smiling. "Now, major, what do you advise?"

"That we march at once along the river road with every man we have, whip the rebels at Stackhouse's, and when that is done, turn back here, and do the same to the other four hundred."

"But, the Rebels in our rear wouldn't stay where they are," said Colonel Kirk. "They would hear the firing, and be down upon us, perhaps before we had flogged those on the river. Thus we might be caught between two superior bodies on that narrow road, where it would be impossible to manœuvre our horses, or to escape, if they proved to be too many for us." "Captain," addressing another officer, "now let us hear from you."

"It seems to me," said this officer, "that the captain and the major have suggested the only two courses that

are open to us. As time is precious I propose that you
put the thing to vote. It will save talk. I shall vote
with Major Rollins."

The majority were in favor of the major's suggestion,
and seeing this he asked the colonel for his decision.

" Before I give it," he said, "I want to ask Mrs. Ellis
a few questions. I have detained you from your bed for
this reason, Mrs. Ellis, but I'll keep you now only a moment longer. How many men did you notice to ride
down the road to act, apparently, as sentries ?"

"I saw only four, sir," she answered. "Some may
have gone before I took notice ; but it's not likely, 'case I
kept my eyes on them."

"And could you see how far they went down the
road ? "

" I watched them turn the first bend in the river below
Stackhouse's," said Phebe, "I couldn't see any further."

"Then they are stretched along the road for a mile or
more," said the colonel. "You said that they stacked
their arms — where did they stack them ?"

" Where the road narrows below Stackhouse's store,
and thar they hitched thar horses. They went ter cooking thar suppers over against the store. I'm sure of that —
I saw some of them go into it for something."

" And the store is about two or three hundred feet
above where they stacked their muskets, and they, no
doubt, went to sleep there," said Colonel Kirk. "Now,
gentlemen, instead of adopting either of your plans, I
will give you a better one. Let Major Rollins get the
men under arms at once, and station all of them in the

rear of this house, except a small squad that he shall post on the hill to observe any movement of the Rebels in the woods.   Meanwhile, I will take a dozen men that I know, and who know me, mount them on our best horses, each one with two sixteen-shooters, two revolvers in his belt, and two in his holster, and will light down on those sleeping fellows at Stackhouse's. We will steal upon the sentinels, and secure them without noise, and then remount, and move softly till we are between the Rebels and their arms, when we will swoop upon them with such yells and firing as will make them think us a whole regiment.   Woke out of sleep by such a din they'll scatter to the four winds — all that are not winged by our carbines or revolvers.   Having done that, we'll toss their stacked arms into the river, and gallop back here, and help you to whip the other four hundred."

"Suppose you don't come back, Colonel?" said the grim-visaged captain. "Suppose the Rebels are not willing to be caught napping?"

"Then we'll take to our heels," answered Colonel Kirk. "It won't be any disgrace for thirteen to run from four hundred. In that case we'll adopt your plan of fighting it out here. Now, gentlemen, each to his command, and get your men ready. We'll make mincemeat of those fellows before morning. Mrs. Ellis, I will show you now to your room, and when this business is over, we will all very heartily thank you for the very great service you have done to us, and the country."

Before two o'clock Colonel Kirk, with his twelve picked men, set out up the river, and by half-past three, he returned, having carried out his programme in the minutest details, without a man so much as wounded. Meanwhile, the four hundred Confederates, whom he had rightly judged to be posted in the woods in his rear, hearing the firing, had moved forward, and engaged the force under Major Rollins. The conflict was at its height, when Kirk returned with his twelve men, and rushed impetuously upon the flank of the Confederates. Probably supposing that his small squad was merely the advance of a larger reinforcement, they fled in all directions, leaving twenty dead, and upwards of thirty wounded upon the ground, and losing a hundred prisoners in the pursuit that followed. This, one of the most brilliant of the minor conflicts of the war, was the last of civil strife in Madison county. The Union forces in the following spring, with Colonel Kirk, and Daniel and Reuben Ellis among them, drove out the Confederates from all the mountain region, but the clash of arms did not come near the blood-stained district which has been the especial scene of this history.

CHAPTER XIV.

CONCLUSION.

It only remains to say a few words in relation to the subsequent career of some of the characters in this history.

Parson Justin had migrated to the adjoining county. Of his life there during the last year of the war I know next to nothing. As the district was then in the hands of the Confederates, he doubtless had no conscientious scruples against openly declaring himself a Disunionist; and he probably kept soul and body together on what remained to him of the "blood-money" he had received for the lives of the sons of Mrs. Hawkins. But when Lee had surrendered, and North Carolina had come under military rule, it became safe for a conscientious man to possess some decided principles. Then the Parson suddenly blossomed out a zealous Loyalist. He went to the military commandant of the district, and gave him an inventory of his losses and sacrifices in the cause of the Union; told him how he had risked his life in aiding unwilling conscripts, and escaped-prisoners, and impoverished himself to feed starving Loyalists; and in confirmation of this last assertion he pointed to the one lean cow, and scanty stock of household goods that comprised his entire worldly possessions. It was the policy of the Government to heal the wounds of the war, and it healed his by a small appointment in the Internal Revenue service.

30

Then Parson Justin throve, and so did the illicit distillers throughout his district. The mountain "moon-
shiners" are noted as ugly customers to handle; but they
never gave the Parson any difficulty. The coon up the
tree said to the famous marksman, Captain Scott, "If
your name is Scott, don't fire, for I'll come down directly."
So the distillers "came down" as the Parson made his
rounds, with his eyes shut, but his hand open.

At last it reached the ears of the Revenue Department
that its trusted official was in league with the law-break-
ers, and the Parson was suddenly asked to render an
account of his stewardship. That he could not conven-
iently do; and, seeing that he was about to be removed,
he resigned in order to save enough reputation to set up
again as a Gospel minister in that mountain region. There,
it may be, he is to-day, preaching the Gospel according to
Justin.

Soon after the close of the war there came to settle in this
mountain region a gentleman from Pittsylvania county,
Virginia, who was acquainted with the culture of tobacco.
He knew that the finest varieties require a soil composed
of a mixture of sand, clay and gravel, an altitude above
the line of eight hundred feet, with a sunny exposure,
cool nights. heavy dews, and an absence of rain in the season of harvest. He found that in this region the meteoric
rocks abound, such as granite, syenite, dionite, and crys-
talline limestone, which give the requisite soil, and that
the other conditions were present in temperate nights, a
copious summer rainfall, and a dry September. At

once he planted a few acres of fresh mountain land with the broad-leaved Oronoko tobacco, and to his surprise, it yielded a luxuriant crop of a variety superior to even the famous "golden-leaf" of Orange, Warren, and Rockingham counties.

The following season he planted a still larger acreage, with even more gratifying results; and then the news spread, and every little farmer with land having a southern exposure, embarked in the raising of tobacco, with the result that his every acre, upon an expenditure of not exceeding fifty dollars, brought him an average return of from one hundred and fifty to three hundred. Farms that might have been bought at three dollars per acre, became suddenly worth all the way from twenty to a hundred dollars, and the whole region was converted into a vast Eldorado — a veritable land of the "golden leaf."

Nearly all of Mrs. Hawkins's extensive plantation had a southern exposure, and the other conditions of soil and climate that are requisite to the successful cultivation of the golden weed. In these circumstances she said one day to Reuben Ellis, "This large plantation is mostly lying idle, while it is capable of yielding such large returns with proper attention. I have no one to leave it to but you and Sukey; and had you not better come here at once, and take its entire management? What land you do not care to cultivate yourself, you can let out to our poor neighbors, who, now that farms here have become so valuable, will soon be driven off from the little places they have squatted upon, by the non-resident owners. They can build themselves little cabins here, and live in peace and contentment. You can put up for yourself another house on the knoll at the east of the barn, so there will not be too many of us in one household; but Robby, as we have agreed, is always to remain with his grandmother.''

In but little more than a year there were all of forty tenant-farmers upon the large plantation, every one of them paying a certain ground-rent per acre, and realizing a return of more than twenty fold as the reward of his industry. Thus it was that Reuben Ellis became a large land-owner, and before many years, the wealthiest man in all that mountain region. Sukey, however, though she was heir to the half of all those broad acres, remained the humble school-mistress; but by dint of hard study she had become so proficient in her profession, that she would, no doubt, have passed examination by even a New England school committee. She took delight in her work, because she saw the children growing up about her intelligent, and respectable men and women; but she took even greater delight, when her school hours were over, in going about from house to house, among the sick and the dying, ministering to their necessities, and discoursing to them of the priceless treasure she had found within the lids of her little Bible — the Almighty Friend, who had given to her, wild and wayward as she had been, and hampered by the heritage of many generations of ignorance and evil, the clear vision of the children of light, and the peace and joy that come to the true Christian. For she had found a truth that is not born of the five senses, and has not so much as entered into the dreams of modern agnosticism.

I made the acquaintance of the lady whom I have styled "Mrs. Hawkins" while journeying on horseback in the summer of 1883, over one of the roughest roads that cross the Southern Alleghanies. I was investigating the early history of the South-west, and tracing the footsteps of John Sevier, who had traversed that wild region in 1782, on his remarkable expedition against the Erati Cherokees. I had journeyed for about eight miles through an almost unbroken forest, which had probably not materially changed its aspect since it was looked upon, a hundred years before, by Nolichucky Jack and his little band of riflemen, when, suddenly, I came upon a broad mountain-side covered with fields of growing tobacco, and dotted, every here and there, almost to the very summit, by trim, well-kept log cottages. On detached knolls on the lower slope of this mountain, and near the high-road, stood two roomy log mansions, surrounded by trees, and covered to the very roof with the clambering Virginia creeper and wild honeysuckle.

Some men were at work in a near-by field, and, halting my horse abreast of them, I inquired who were the occupants of the two mansions. They told me that the mansions, and about all the land I could see, were the property of the persons I have called Reuben Ellis and Mrs. Hawkins; and they further said that the lady would deem a call from me no intrusion, for she kept open-house to everybody, and especially to strangers. Thereupon,

having already heard much of her, I rode up to the nearer
of the two mansions, and encountered the lady whose life
I have imperfectly detailed in this volume.

Mrs. Hawkins pressed me to dine with her, and at dinner I met a well-dressed, well-mannered, and intelligent
young man of about twenty-five, and a comely, vivacious,
and remarkably agreeable woman, whose hair was slightly
touched with gray, and who laughingly told me that she
was too old to catch a beau, seeing that she was past fifty.
The young man was the little fellow, Robby, who cared
for his younger brother the night and day that his mother
was away on her perilous trip to Kirk's head-quarters;
and the comely middle-aged woman was Sukey.

After dinner Sukey invited me into her school-room,
where about fifty boys and girls had gathered from the
recess they were accustomed to take during the family's
dinner-hour; and when I came to ride away, Mrs. Hawkins urged me to come again, and to bring with me the
ladies of my household. This I did again and again, and
I never came away without having received from this lady
some ideas that were worth pondering; for she had a
clear, comprehensive mind, and her very isolation from
the world had seemed to give her the ability to take broad,
bird's-eye views of things. On one of these occasions
she gave me some thoughts which may form a fitting conclusion to this history.

Slavery, she said, had before the war become so inter-
twined with the social system of the South, and the mon-
eyed interests of the North, that it could not be extirpated
without a convulsion that should shake the nation from

centre to circumference. It was inconsistent with our character as a free people, and it had to be brought to an end, or our country would miss its destiny as the apostle to all the world of civil and religious liberty. But how could it be brought to an end, with the North content to let it alone, and its continued existence secured to the South by the Constitution? How, except by the mad folly of the slave-holders themselves. A parasite had grown up around the oak, and this parasite, carefully tended and fostered by the slave-aristocracy, was that which had at last strangled the gigantic evil.

This parasite was States Rights. It originated from the fact that the Thirteen Colonies, though all under the Dominion of Great Britain, had each a separate and independent existence. The war of the Revolution forced them into a union; but it was a union as States and not as a people. The Confederacy they formed had neither strength nor vitality, and it fell to pieces of its own weakness. Then the *people* formed the Constitution, and by it made of the Union a Nation. This was the view of the North, which held that this Union was indissoluble and perpetual. The view of the South was the opposite. It held that the Union was merely a league between sovereign States, each of which could resume its sovereignty at its pleasure. The two views were irreconcilable, and one or the other had to prevail the moment a single State seceded. The slave-holders well understood this, and that the Southern people would fight for State rights, and thus they hoped to protect and perpetuate slavery.

And the Southern people did fight for States Rights, and not for the three hundred and eighty thousand slave-holders who forced them into secession. Their leaders were blind and wicked; but the people themselves were merely misled and mistaken, and hence there is no word of blame for them — nothing but admiration for their bravery in defeat, and their constancy in misfortune. We should welcome them back with all fraternal feeling, proud to have them again as brothers, and to be allowed to build up with them, hand in hand, our great nation.

Destructive as the war was, the country, both South and North, has gained by it immeasurably. It has removed forever all possible cause for dissension and disunion; it has won for us the admiration of the world, and demonstrated that republican institutions have in them an enduring strength and vitality; and it has given the two sections a mutual respect for each other, which, more than any thing else, will cement them together in a Union which shall be perpetual. In another hundred years the English-speaking race will be the controlling element in the world, and then it will be seen why in the Providence of God, we have been preserved as one people, and built up into a vast and united nation. These thoughts, together with the larger part of the details which are embodied in the foregoing narrative, I had from the lady I have herein styled Mrs. Hawkins.

THE END.

www.ingramcontent.com/pod-product-compliance
Lightning Source LLC
Chambersburg PA
CBHW020104030726
47498CB00006B/1942